CLOWNFISH

CLOWNFISH

CLOWNFISH

Alan Durant

WALKER
BOOKS

First published in Great Britain 2018 by Walker Books Ltd
87 Vauxhall Walk, London SE11 5HJ

2 4 6 8 10 9 7 5 3 1

Text © 2018 Alan Durant
Cover art and illustrations by Helen Crawford-White

Excerpts from "Sea Fever" by John Masefield reprinted by permission of The Society of Authors as the Literary Representative of the Estate of John Masefield.

Excerpts from "For the Union Dead" from COLLECTED POEMS by Robert Lowell. Copyright © 2003 by Harriet Lowell and Sheridan Lowell. Reprinted by permission of Farrar, Straus and Giroux.

Every reasonable effort has been made to trace ownership of and/or secure permission for the use of copyrighted material. If notified of any omission, the author and publisher will gladly make the necessay correction on future reprints.

The right of Alan Durant to be identified as author of this work has been asserted by him in accordance with the Copyright, Designs and Patents Act 1988

This book has been typeset in Utopia

Printed and bound by CPI Group (UK) Ltd, Croydon CR0 4YY

British Library Cataloguing in Publication Data:
a catalogue record for this book is
available from the British Library

ISBN 978-1-4063-7462-9

www.walker.co.uk

MIX
Paper from
responsible sources
FSC® C020471

To my dad,

Christopher Durant (1929–2016),

with love always and forever

"You miss your dad,
don't you, Sharkbait?"

Gill, *Finding Nemo*

"What's it like, Dad – being a fish?"

It was something I'd wanted to ask him for a while and, as he was still for once and the aquarium was quiet, this seemed a good time.

Dad looked up with a startled twitch and swished over to me. His little mouth opened and shut as if he was considering the question carefully.

"Wet," he said at last.

"But is it … fun? Are you *happy*?"

"Fun? Happy? Well, it beats sorting other people's rubbish, I suppose." Dad had worked at the recycling centre before he turned into a fish. "It's very busy."

"Is it? What do you do all day?"

He gave a kind of flick, like a fish shrug. "Swim around the tank, chase the damselfish, eat, blow bubbles, lie in my anemone, swim around the tank..."

"You already said that."

Dad pouted. "Did I? My memory's not as good as it was."

"That's 'cos you're a fish, Dad." I smiled. "It must be great living here in the aquarium with all these other amazing fish. Every morning you can wake up and see the rays." The rays had always been our favourites. They'd flap to the surface, raising their strange flat heads, as if begging to be stroked, then flipping over. Some felt rough, others slimy. They had little bumps down their back you could run your fingers along as they flapped by, as if you were playing a musical instrument.

"Oh, the rays!" Dad said dismissively. "Just show-offs, they are. You don't want to waste your time on them."

"But, Dad!" I was shocked. "You loved the rays. 'Rays of sunshine', you called them. You used to talk to them, remember? You said they could understand every word."

"Ah, well, I wasn't a fish then. I've got an inside view now, haven't I? And I'll tell you something for free: rays are just about the dumbest fish in the entire ocean.

The other fish are always making fun of them. You should hear the jokes they tell."

"Really? Like what?"

Dad thought for a moment. "What do you call a clever ray?"

"I don't know," I said. "What do you call a clever ray?"

"A flounder."

I pulled a face. "I don't get it."

"Well, there's no such thing as a clever ray, is there? So if it's clever, it must be a flounder – another sort of flat fish. See?"

"Oh." I frowned. "It's not very funny, is it?"

Dad waggled irritatedly. "You have to be a fish to appreciate the joke. Fish have a very particular sense of humour."

"Yeah, I can see that," I said.

He swished to the front of the tank, glancing quickly from side to side as if checking we were alone, then waved his fins at me to come closer. "You haven't got a burger on you by any chance, have you?" he whispered.

I shook my head.

He sighed. "Well, maybe next time." Then he yawned. "Anyway, look, I'm off to have a rest in my anemone. It's beautiful in there, you know. Beautiful!

It's like diving into the fluffiest shag-pile rug you could imagine. You should try it some time."

Dad waddled away, then turned and waddled back.

"Only, on second thoughts," he added, in a serious, fatherly tone, "its tentacles are poisonous, so you'd better stay away. One dea—" He hesitated. "One *fish* in the family is quite enough."

It all started like this.

One morning Dad was eating breakfast and Mum was making tea. I'd already left for school. Dad's always joking and fooling around. It's one of the things that I love about him. Sometimes it drove Mum mad – which was probably why she didn't take his gasping seriously at first.

He'd just taken a bite of toast (carefully spread with butter, a thin layer of Marmite and a smothering of strawberry jam – his own favourite "concoction", as he called it) when he began coughing … then gasping. Mum thought it was just – well, Dad being Dad. But then he crashed face down onto the kitchen table and she knew something was seriously wrong. She called an ambulance, but by the time it arrived, Dad was completely still, with no heartbeat, no pulse, no breath. The paramedics tried to revive him, but there was nothing they could do. Dad had suffered a massive heart attack.

He was dead. Gone… Or so it seemed.

I just couldn't take in what had happened. It didn't seem real. That morning when I'd gone to school, Dad had been there, joking as usual, pulling silly faces, doing daft voices, looking forward to a day at home; later, when I came back, he was dead. Where was the sense in that?

I couldn't cry. I couldn't feel anything. It was all so weird: Mum's pale face and her sobbing; the constant flow of people through the house, asking me questions: *Was I OK? Did I want to talk to someone?* Of course I did – I wanted to talk to Dad. I wanted him to walk in the front door laughing at the joke he'd pulled on all of us. I wanted him to wink at me like he always did and say, "Got you there, Dak."

I thought the funeral might change things, but it didn't. It just made everything seem even less real. At the crematorium, a priest I'd never seen before said a few words about Dad. *Robert had a great sense of humour*, he said. *He'll be greatly missed by all who knew him.* For a moment I didn't take in who he was talking about. Nobody ever called Dad "Robert". He was Bob or, sometimes, Bobby, but never Robert. The whole thing was wrong.

When the coffin started to slide away, it was to the Hallelujah Chorus, which I'd heard Dad sing loads of times – but always in a ridiculous opera-style voice as a joke. Never straight, as it was played here.

Afterwards people shook my hand and said what a tragedy it was, how sorry they were, how brave I was being. I didn't feel brave. I still didn't feel anything. It was like there was a glass barrier between me and what was taking place. This barrier only slid aside once: when I looked up to see, in clear focus, grey smoke puffing from the crematorium chimneys. I had this sudden sharp ache, like my heart was wincing, and I quickly looked down again.

That night I went into Mum and Dad's room and found one of his favourite sweatshirts – rain-cloud grey with a yellow smiley – from the chest of drawers. I took it to bed with me, breathing in its familiar Dad smell, hugging it like a blankie to try to conjure him, in the desperate hope that it would bring him to life again, like in those sci-fi films when they manage to clone someone from just a strand of their DNA.

But Dad wasn't coming back, was he? He wasn't going to come into my room and ruffle my hair or crack a joke, or kiss me goodnight. I'd never see his face or hear his voice again, I thought. I pressed the sweatshirt against my damp eyes.

Dad was gone. For ever.

When I got up the next day, I knew I had to get away from the house. I'd been cooped up too long. I was tired of visitors whose presence just seemed to make Dad's absence more unbearable. They weren't even family. Mum and Dad didn't have any siblings and nor did I. Our only relative was Mum's mum, my grandmother, who lived on the other side of the world. The visitors were family friends or neighbours like Mrs Baxter from up the road, who was with Mum now.

I didn't like Mrs Baxter – I didn't want her there, taking charge as if it was her home. I just wanted Dad. Couldn't anyone understand that? All I wanted was Dad – funny, crazy, lovable, wonderful Dad.

I didn't even want to talk to my friends. I had two best friends at school – Ruby and Tom. We often met up at weekends – went round to each other's houses or to the beach or the shopping centre. I liked them a lot. But after what happened to Dad, I couldn't speak to them. I didn't want to see them. I was sure that they'd ask me questions and pity me like all the others and I couldn't stand the thought of that.

They tried calling and emailing; they wanted to come round and see me, they said, but I wouldn't let them. My head felt too crammed full for other people, even my friends – *especially* my friends. So I avoided them and ignored their efforts to contact and comfort me. Ruby came round one day, but I didn't open the door. I pretended no one was home. I felt bad about doing it, but I just couldn't face seeing her. Not then.

That morning, after the funeral, I escaped to the aquarium. It was only a short walk away, down by the beach, and the breezy air did me good. I chose the aquarium because it had been Dad's favourite place and I loved it too. We went so often that Dad had bought a family season ticket. Now I could go whenever I liked.

Dad and Stephan, the owner, had known each other for ages, they'd gone to the same secondary school. They were always chatting about the old days – friends they'd shared, things they'd done. That's when they weren't talking about fish. They both loved fish. Dad used to say they were "ichthyophiles". Well, actually he said they were, "*hic*-thyophiles". He said it like he had hiccups. I always smiled but Stephan didn't. He had sort of droopy eyes and a whiskery saggy face that made him look permanently miserable.

Cheer up, Stephan, it may never happen, Dad used to say.

It already has, Bob, was Stephan's gloomy reply.

"Dak, I didn't expect to see you," he said now, with surprise, as I pushed open the glass doors and entered the aquarium. "How are you?"

"Fine," I mumbled. I felt uncomfortable in the bright light of the foyer. I wanted the murky anonymity of the aquarium's main hall.

Stephan ran his fingers over the thin, sandy-grey moustache that hung down at either side of his mouth like a fish's barbels. "I still can't get over it, about your dad. It's terrible. Terrible."

I nodded. I liked Stephan a lot but I really didn't want to talk. I just didn't know what to say, so I shuffled quickly away.

I loved all the fish in the aquarium. There was something fascinating about every one of them – name, colour, features, movement, habits – though today I was too busy with my own thoughts to pay them much attention. I wandered through their world, deep in my own. I felt a lot closer to Dad here than I had at home or at the funeral. I could see him now, peering into some tank with amused excitement, calling out to me to join him: "Come and see this, Dak. This'll make you smile."

Together we'd watch the spotted garden eels, poking up out of the sand like thin silver periscopes, stretching, bending, swaying, one moment hardly visible, the next weirdly tall. Or the flashlight fish with its fluorescent white eye that winked in the darkness. Or the bug-eyed Picasso triggerfish, or the fox-face rabbitfish, or the stripy lionfish with its exotic and deadly skirts. If Dad's spirit was anywhere, I was sure it wasn't in the cemetery, but here in the aquarium among the fish he loved.

As I passed through the Coral Reef section, images of Dad floated before me like the bubbles from a fish's mouth. He was everywhere … but he was gone. *Forever.*

The realisation was like a punch in the stomach. I felt suddenly dizzy, faint with loss, and slumped down on a chair, closing my eyes and taking long, slow breaths, waiting for my heart to steady, for the pain to fade…

"Dak? Dak!"

The voice was urgent, impatient. I opened my eyes slowly, thinking it would stop, but it didn't.

"Dak!" it called again, more sharply. It seemed to be coming from the tank beside me. Turning my head, I saw small purply-blue fish with amber tails, and green fish darting about clumps of reddy-brown coral.

I peered at the identification labels at the base of the glass: *Pomacentrus melanochir*, **Blue-finned damsel**, and *Chromis caerulea*, **Green chromis**. (Stephan always put the fish's Latin name first; it sounded more dignified, he'd explained when I had once asked him why.) There was an anemone listed too, a sea hedgehog, and one other fish. I examined the card and photograph more closely: *Amphiprion percula*, **Clownfish**.

As I glanced up it approached me through the water, orangey-red with wide bands of white. "Dak," it said, wagging its thin face as if it was a bit cross. For a moment, we were eye to eye.

My mouth gaped open.

"Speak to me," the fish demanded. "Say something, anything – as long as it's not Shakespeare. Or the shipping forecast. Them, I can live without."

My mouth gaped wider. For an instant all I could do was grunt *"ahh"* as if I was at the doctor's having my throat examined.

Finally, I managed a single, quavery "Dad?" – then, "Dad, is that you?"

The clownfish swished itself one way, then the other. "Of course it's me," it said, laughing. "Who did you think it was … a fish?"

2

So that's how it happened – how I discovered my dad hadn't died, but turned into a clownfish at the aquarium. It was amazing, astonishing, incredible – wonderful! My dad was alive and talking to me!

There were so many things I wanted to say, but I couldn't speak. I just stood there grinning. Dad wanted to know what kind of fish he was. "Not a perch! Tell me I'm not a perch! Or an eel. Anything but that."He shivered theatrically.

I shook my head. "You're neither of those. You're a clownfish."

Dad wobbled his head and chuckled, shooting a jet of bubbles through the water. "A clownfish!" he gurgled. "A clownfish!" He chased after a chromis that was swimming close by, then flimflammed back to the front of the tank.

"What are you doing, Dad?" I asked.

"Oh, you know, just having some fun. Clowning around." He waggled his little flipper fins and rolled his black beady eyes, pouting ridiculously.

"You're crazy, Dad," I laughed. I felt my heart leap back into life. "I knew you weren't really dead, I just knew it."

The clownfish wiggled in the water. "Me, dead?" he said. "No way, mate. I'm alive and kicking, I am. Well, alive and flipping anyway."

I stared at the clownfish. I still couldn't take this all in. "But how did it happen? How did you become a fish?"

Dad waggled his flippers again, as if in a shrug. "Search me, son. One moment I was eating breakfast in the kitchen, the next I was here. Like magic."

I nodded. It *was* magic, wasn't it? My dad hadn't died. He'd turned into a living, breathing, talking fish! And here I was, chatting with him.

"A clownfish," Dad said, his little mouth sort of smiling, "like Nemo. I remember watching that film with you when you were very small. It was your favourite – *Finding Nemo*. You watched it over and over... I think you knew the whole film by heart."

23

"Yeah, I did." I laughed.

"You didn't like the anglerfish, though," Dad continued. "You thought it was freaky."

The anglerfish always made me shiver. I was glad there wasn't one in the aquarium.

"You didn't like that bit at the start, either, when the barracuda—"

"Nobody likes that bit, Dad," I interrupted. "The bit I like best is when Nemo and his dad are reunited. Like us."

Dad flicked his tail and pouted. "Nemo's dad's nothing like me. I never lost *my* son," he said huffily. "And he wouldn't know a good joke if it bit him." He gave me a frowny dark-eyed stare. "With fronds like you who needs anemones," he mimicked. "Even a ray could come up with a better joke than that." And he swished away.

I waited for a while, hoping he'd come back, but it seemed he'd had enough for now. I didn't mind too much. He wasn't going anywhere, was he? He'd still be there when I came back. This was his home now – and I could visit him whenever I wanted.

I almost danced back to the house that afternoon. The first thing I saw when I got there was Becks, the stone bulldog. He was sitting in the front garden wearing a pink plastic rain hat. Dad had rescued him from the recycling centre and brought him home. He was as good as new, except that he'd lost one ear.

Mum thought Becks was ugly and ridiculous, but Dad had insisted on putting him on our tiny front lawn. One sunny day, as a joke, he'd placed a straw boater (also rescued from the dump) on Becks's head. People stopped and looked and laughed. After that, Dad gave the dog a variety of hats and accessories. Depending on the weather and the time of year, Becks wore a tartan bobble hat and scarf, a Father Christmas hat and red cape, a Union Jack sunhat and rainbow sunglasses, an old tin army helmet...

As I passed Becks, I whipped off the rain hat. I'd swap it for the Union Jack sun hat that was stored with the other hats in the front porch. That was Dad's hat for special occasions – and today I had something really special to celebrate, didn't I? I pulled the pink hat down over my head and grinned at the stone bulldog.

The front door opened and Doctor Doyle appeared. She was wearing a black and white checked skirt with a green cardigan, and carried a large black bag. She was tall and standing on the top step, she looked like a giantess.

"So there you are, young man," she said with a frown. "Your mother was worried about you. She didn't know where you were."

"I went out for a bit," I gabbled, quickly taking off the rain hat. "Mrs Baxter was here. I didn't think they'd notice I was gone."

"Well, your mum did notice and she was worried."

"I went to the aquarium," I said meekly. I certainly hadn't meant to upset Mum and I was surprised that I had. She'd barely seemed to notice me over the last few days.

"You must tell your mum before you go off. She's very anxious right now and needs to avoid any undue stress." Doctor Doyle came down the stairs. She bent down so that she and I were face to face. "She's really quite ill, you know, Dak; she needs a lot of looking after."

I nodded. "I'll look after her," I said. I was twelve, soon to go into my second year of secondary school. I wasn't a little kid any more.

Doctor Doyle smiled. "But what about you, Dak?"

"I'm fine. I can look after myself."

The doctor looked doubtful. "Are you sure?

"Yes," I said firmly.

Of course I was fine. I was better than fine. I was

happy. Who wouldn't be happy to discover that the dad he loved and thought was dead wasn't dead after all – he'd simply turned into a tropical fish? But I knew it would be a waste of time trying to tell the doctor that; she'd just pity me more.

I didn't want her pity. I didn't need it. Why, on such a happy day, would I need anyone's pity?

I went up to see Mum – she was lying on the bed with her head propped up on a couple of pillows. Her eyes were open, staring, and they were so full of misery that I felt a stab of shame.

"Mum," I called softly. "I'm back."

Mum moved her head towards me but her expression didn't change. There was neither anger nor relief – only misery. I sat beside her on the bed and she reached out a hand to me. I leant against her and felt the downy softness of her sweater on my cheek, smelt the familiar sweet vanilla of her perfume.

"Oh, Dak," she moaned. "Oh, Dak."

I put my arms around her and squeezed gently. "It's okay, Mum," I murmured. "I'll look after you."

I longed to tell her the amazing news about Dad. But I sensed that it wasn't the right moment. I'd only upset her more – and I couldn't bear that. It would have to be my secret until she was stronger and ready to share it.

"I'll make you a cup of tea," I offered brightly. In times of stress, Dad always suggested tea.

While the kettle boiled, I went out to the front lawn and put the Union Jack sun hat on Becks. I imagined the clownfish waddling towards me and I smiled.

3

I dreamed of the Isle of Wight.

I was at a theme park with Dad. Dad was on the pirate ship, pretending to be a pirate. He was saying crazy things like *Avast, me smarties!* and *Hoist the skull and crossbuns!* I was laughing my head off, having a great time. But then, suddenly, a gang of real pirates swarmed from nowhere onto the ship. They captured Dad and me. We were out at sea and there were sharks and giant barracudas in the water, lots of them. The pirates were making Dad walk the plank. Three more steps and he'd be in the water.

I had to do something to save him – but I couldn't move. I tried to cry out, but I had no voice.

"Aagh!"

I woke, gasping. Rain pattered on the attic skylight

like the panicky beating of my heart. I shut my eyes, reached for the old grey sweatshirt … and remembered: Dad was alive; Dad was a clownfish safe in the aquarium. Everything was OK.

That morning I put the sweatshirt back under the pillow, got up and dressed. Mum was still sleeping. The tablets she took knocked her out completely and she probably wouldn't surface for an hour or so yet. I wrote her a note and left it on the bedside table so that she wouldn't worry.

It was barely raining, just "picking" as Dad would say, speckling black dots on the concrete path. (He loved words that sounded a bit funny like "picking" and "concoction" and "flimflam" and "lugubrious" – and now, so did I.) It wasn't wet enough to change Becks's headgear. Not that I would have changed the Union Jack sun hat anyway, even if it had been chucking it down.

The aquarium was just opening. "You're an early bird," Stephan greeted me.

"Mmm," I agreed, heading quickly for the door that led to the tunnel into the main hall.

I was thinking about my dream. I'd gone on holiday with Mum and Dad to the Isle of Wight last summer. One day we went to a theme park called

Blackgang Chine. Dad was in his element. He enjoyed the place even more than me. We had a mock gunfight in a cowboy saloon and Dad threw up his hands as if he'd been shot and dropped to his knees, moaning and groaning ridiculously. Then we joined the crew of a pirate ship.

But it hadn't been at all scary like it was in my dream. We had brilliant fun. Dad stood on the poop deck shouting, *Ahoy, there, shipmates!* and *Shiver me timbers!* and *Who's nicked me parrot?* I really laughed at that.

On the Isle of Wight, we'd also gone to an aquarium. It wasn't as big as Stephan's and looked a bit old, like it might fall to pieces at any moment. The tanks were grimy and had pieces of sticky tape on them and there were pipes snaking all over the place, but it had plenty of interesting fish. On each tank there was a funny little notice about the creatures inside, typewritten on a scrap of card: `This is a moray eel. You won't be able to smell it, but it can certainly smell you! Moray eels have a keener sense of smell than a police sniffer dog.`

I remembered that now. I remembered the eel too – it was greeny-yellow like a tennis ball. It kept opening and shutting its mouth as if it was shouting, "Help!"

I reminded Dad about it. "'Feed me!', more like."
He laughed. "They're greedy beggars, those eels." He
wagged his stripy head. "The word in here is that one
of them got so greedy the other day he swallowed
himself."

I shook my head. "That's rubbish, Dad. How could
a fish eat itself?"

"I'm just telling you what I heard," said Dad grump-
ily. "Mind you, it was a liar fish that told me." A jet of
laughter bubbled from his mouth.

I shook my head. "*You're* the liar fish."

When I told Dad about my dream, he told me not
to worry. "There are no sharks or barracudas in this
tank," he assured me. "Just me, the clownfish, and the
chromis and the damselfish."

I reminded him that there had been clownfish in
that aquarium on the Isle of Wight. I had never seen
a real one before – only the animated ones in *Finding
Nemo* – and it had been love at first sight. When we
came home, I'd persuaded Stephan to get one.

They're great examples of symbiosis, I'd said, quot-
ing from the card on the tank at the Isle of Wight
aquarium. Clownfish make their home among
sea anemones, whose tentacles are poisonous to most fish.

"The only thing I didn't tell Stephan," I said to Dad now, "is that clownfish can be a bit aggressive."

"Me, aggressive?" said Dad indignantly. Then he took a chomp at a passing damselfish.

"Dad!"

"Only joking," he sniggered. "You've got to laugh, haven't you? Or … well, you've just got to laugh, that's all."

He faced the front of the tank, his little black eyes staring out at me.

"Want to hear an eel joke?" he asked suddenly.

"All right," I said.

"What did the shark sing when it met a family of eels swimming across the ocean?"

"I don't know. What did it sing?"

"Eel meat again," Dad sung. His pink lips twitched in a quick smile. "Have a good day, son. I'll see you later … *eel*-igator."

Then with a *swish-swash*, he swam back to his anemone.

4

I went to the aquarium every day – I arrived at opening time and was the last customer to leave. I'd happily have stayed there all night.

"I ought to make up a bed for you," Stephan said. "Is your mother all right with you being here so much?"

"It's fine," I assured him. "She sleeps most of the time."

Stephan nodded sympathetically. "It must be very hard for her."

I spent all day chatting with Dad or watching him swish around the tank. We shared happy memories and he'd tell me about his life as a fish. Overall, apart from the food, he seemed to be content.

"Don't you miss your old life – as a human?" I asked him.

"Nah," he replied. "It's much more relaxing here. I don't have to work, I get fed regularly and no one gives me grief."

"Who gave you grief before?"

"Oh, you know, people down at the tip who put their rubbish in the wrong container and then got shirty if you told them." He thought for a moment. "And Mum sometimes."

"Mum?"

Dad twitched. "Oh, just when I sat on the sofa in my dirty overalls. That sort of thing."

I smiled. "No, she didn't like you doing that."

"Or when I played one of my jokes on her. She gave me grief then all right."

"But only for a moment," I said quickly. "She always forgave you, didn't she?"

"Oh, yes, your mum can take a joke," Dad said. He wobbled with amusement. "Well, she must do. She took me."

I decided not to tell him about Mum – how ill and unhappy she was. What good would it do? He couldn't do anything in here, could he? It would only upset him.

Another of the things Dad had brought home from the dump was a singing fish called Trevor the Rainbow

Trout. It was a large colourful plastic fish mounted on a wooden board. He'd cleaned it up and put it on top of the bathroom toilet. When anyone went near the toilet it started to sing this old song.

I'd laughed out loud the first time it had suddenly turned its head towards me and sung, "Wild thing, you make my heart sing!" It flicked its tail out to the beat too. It had been even funnier when Mum sat on the toilet and the fish started singing. She screamed and Dad and I slapped hands outside the bathroom door. She gave Dad grief for that – but not for long. She was soon laughing with us.

Over the next months that fish astonished many people, especially when its motor went wrong and its voice took on a weird spooky tone like it had been possessed by a demon. Eventually it died completely and not even a new battery could revive it. Dad hadn't thrown it out though. He left it lying soundless, motionless on the top of the toilet as if he hoped someday it might return to life and burst into song again.

One morning Stephan found me by the clownfish tank. Dad was resting on his anemone, while the damsels and chromis flickered through the water.

Stephan said he had a proposition for me. He

wanted to know if I'd help Johnny, his assistant, with the feeding – the boy who used to help had moved away.

"So Johnny's a bit stuck," Stephan said. "It's hard for him to give his talk and do the feeding too. He could do with a helper and I was wondering if you'd be interested, Dak – seeing as you're here so much."

I grinned. "Yes! Yes, please!" I said excitedly.

This was perfect. Now I'd have a reason to be here – a reason other people would understand and encourage. Things were getting better and better...

I had my first feeding session with Johnny that afternoon. I knew who he was but we'd never spoken before. I'd always thought he looked a bit scary.

"All right, mate." Johnny smiled when, hesitantly, I introduced myself. "Good to see ya." He was dressed in black, as always, from head to toe. His hair was slicked into a quiff at the front and his ears were riddled with piercings. There was a tattoo of some kind of crab on the left side of his neck. "Stephan says you're up for helping us."

"Yes," I nodded. My voice sounded small and croaky.

"Ya sure?" Johnny asked. I nodded again, more vigorously. I didn't want him to think I wasn't keen.

"That's great," Johnny continued. "There ain't much to it really. Ya just gotta drop the food in when I give ya the nod."

The sea bass were first. Johnny showed me the food and how much I needed to put in the tank. "Ya don't care about getting a bit wet, do ya?" he asked cheerfully.

"No," I answered, a little puzzled. I wasn't actually going in the tank, was I?

"They can be a bit frisky," Johnny said, as if that explained everything.

Feeding time for the sea bass was two o'clock. A small group of adults and children gathered around the tank. Johnny advised them not to get too close – which made me a little anxious. Why did everyone have to stand back – everyone except me, that was? I looked into the tank: the stocky silvery-grey sea bass were bobbing around lazily. The tank was fuller than most in the aquarium, but the fish didn't look scary at all.

"Ready then, mate?" Johnny asked me – and I nodded. "Good," he said. He turned to face the audience. "Good afternoon, ladies and gents, boys and girls and—" he gestured to the tank— "fish, of course." There was a ripple of laughter. "In a moment or two ya gonna witness the feeding of these fine fellas here, namely the sea bass." He waved his hand again. "Now, does anyone know anything about sea bass?"

"I know they're delicious pan-fried with fennel," said a man with a small child on his shoulders and there was another ripple of laughter.

Johnny nodded. "Well, it's interesting ya should say that, mate," he said good-humouredly, "'cos most people probably only think of sea bass as something on their plate. They're a very popular fish for food – and for sport. So popular, in fact, that they had to be made a protected species. The law says if ya catch more than two in a day then you have to throw the rest back into the sea, where they belong." Johnny looked around, addressing his whole audience as he talked. His final comment, however, was directed very specifically at the man who'd spoken, who gave a small, shame-faced nod.

I'd been right, I reckoned, to be a bit scared of Johnny. He seemed jolly enough, but there was a steely edge to him. I watched now as he went on to explain with relaxed expertise that the sea bass was not one particular fish, but the name given to any of the 475 species of the family Serranidae ("hamlet, hind, cony, graysby, jewfish, groupers, to name but a few") most of which were to be found in the shallower waters of warm and tropical seas.

"Sea bass vary widely in size," he continued, "from a few centimetres to a maximum of two metres and two hundred and twenty-five kilograms." He acted the measurements out first with his thumb and forefinger, then with a dramatic sweep of his arms. "That's five hundred pounds in old money, madam," he added cheekily to an elderly woman holding the hand of a small boy – her grandson, I guessed. "The majority of fish in this tank are groupers. They ain't the most dynamic of fish, but that'll change in a moment when young Dak, my intrepid assistant here, gives 'em their grub."

The small boy raised his hand. "What do they eat?" he asked.

Johnny crouched down with a warm smile. "Good question, son – *very* good question. Well, sea bass are carnivorous, like us. They feed on small fish, crustaceans like shrimps, and molluscs – clams, sea snails, that sort of thing. We give 'em a kind of fishy mix that contains all the goodness they need and they seem to like it all right – as you'll see." He grinned broadly, which made him look even scarier. "And now, if there's no more questions, we'll get on with the main event." He raised one pierced eyebrow at me. "All set?"

I nodded. Johnny turned back to his audience.

"Okay, I'm gonna count to three and then I want ya all to shout 'Feed the fish!', nice and loud – and Dak here will do the honours." I held the bucket of fish food a little in front of me. Its smell definitely wasn't appetizing – strong, sharp, a bit like wee.

"One, two, three…!" cried Johnny.

"Feed the fish!" the audience responded enthusiastically.

I poured the mix into the tank – and the sleepy, lazy fish came suddenly to life in a fluster of mouths, fins and tails. They squirmed wildly, their tails slapping the surface, splashing water out of the tank. I stepped back quickly but not before I'd been soaked from head to foot. The audience laughed.

Johnny shook his head and his quiff bounced. "And that, ladies and gents, is why ya don't wanna get too close at feeding time – 'specially not in mating season. As ya can see, they get a little frisky." I wiped the drips of water off my face with my hand. "Now I think we should give my assistant a clap, don't you? That was his very first feeding time and he did a great job."

He started to applaud and the audience joined in. I smiled weakly.

* * *

"Well done, mate," Johnny congratulated me when everyone had gone. "Soz you got wet, but it's a good end to the show."

"It's OK." I shrugged. "I don't mind a bit of water."

"Good man," said Johnny and he punched me lightly on the shoulder. "I reckon ya gonna be just fine."

5

That night I had more uncomfortable dreams. I woke wet with sweat and, as before, it took me some time to recover and get everything back into perspective. I rubbed my face into Dad's old sweatshirt, took a deep breath, felt its soft familiarity slowly soothe me…

I washed and dressed, then went into Mum's bedroom and was surprised to find her awake. She called me to her for a hug.

"Are you OK, Dak?" she asked, her arms wrapped around me.

"I'm fine, Mum. You don't have to worry about me."

"But I do," she sighed. "I do worry, Dak. I worry about everything." She hugged me so tightly it was like she was trying to bring me back inside her. I closed my eyes and smelt her warm, sleepy scent. She kissed

43

my head and I felt her start to sob, tears wetting my forehead.

I was a bit guilty because I still hadn't said anything about Dad. That would stop her tears right away, wouldn't it? Or would it? I lifted my head and put my hands on her face softly.

"It'll be all right, Mum," I whispered. I kissed her on the cheek and went to make her a cup of tea.

I didn't go straight to the aquarium that morning – I stopped off at the beach first, crunching over the pebbles between the salt-weathered wooden groynes and sitting down where the beach banked. It was still too early for tourists, which meant that the gulls were either high in the sky or scavenging in the town.

Dad always used to complain about them, when he was on bin duty, before he started working at the recycling centre. "Nasty great scavengers", he called them. If you left a black rubbish sack out for the binmen then the seagulls would split it and scatter the trash across the street. *And who do you think has to clear that up?* Dad said indignantly.

He complained about their pooping too. Every car had seagull poop on it somewhere. Dad was always out in the street with a cloth and a scraper trying to get poop off his car. Mind you, I didn't see why he bothered – the car was an old piece of junk anyway, an ancient orangey-red Volkswagen Beetle, that Dad called a "classic motor" and I nicknamed "The Wreck". It was always breaking down, which made Mum mad. *That thing's going to drive me to an early grave*, she'd said.

You'd have to get it started first, I'd laughed.

But Dad wouldn't hear a word against "Gertie". He gave the car that name because it sounded "sort of dignified", he said. *No matter what you do in life, you have to have dignity, Dak*, he told me.

He never explained exactly what he meant by the word, but I think it had something to do with respecting yourself and gaining the respect of others, even if you did work at the rubbish tip and drive an old banger – or stand by a fish tank in an aquarium, like me, soaking wet…

I didn't get so wet the second time I fed the sea bass, though – wet enough that the audience laughed, but not dripping from head to toe. I got a laugh when we fed the rays and the small sharks too – but only because I made a bit of a mess of it. I was using a pair of feeding tongs, which we needed (as Johnny explained to the audience) because the sharks were faster than the rays and would eat all the food if it was just thrown into the tank. With the tongs, I could feed the fish individually and make sure they all got their fair share.

That was the idea anyway. I was a bit hopeless at first and let the sprat I was holding out to a ray slide out of the pincers too early straight into the mouth of a delighted shark. Luckily Johnny was busy warning a woman not to touch the thornback rays and didn't notice.

Like his bass talk, Johnny's chat was a mix of facts and conservation. He told the audience that rays and sharks were related. That they had cartilage but no bones. That they didn't have scales either, but were covered in hundreds of backward-facing teeth.

"Shark's skin's so rough that back in the past carpenters used to use it as sandpaper," he said, shaking his head in disapproval. Then, more cheerily, he asked, "Now does anyone here like to go to the chippy?" Lots of hands shot up, lured into his trap. "Well, you'll see some of these fellas on the menu as rock salmon or hasse. And yet, rays, like a lot of fish, are under threat from overfishing."

I was glad I'd never eaten rock salmon. I'd have felt terrible.

At the end of the afternoon, on my way home from the aquarium, I went to the supermarket, taking money out from the cashpoint to pay. I'd got money out for Mum before, so I knew her PIN. She didn't know I had her card so I felt a little guilty, but we needed food and there was nothing in the house. I bought some baked beans, eggs, bread and milk – and a bar of Mum's favourite chocolate. She probably wouldn't eat it, but I hoped it might cheer her up a little.

When I got home Mrs Baxter was there, bustling between the kitchen and the dining room. She was standing in the hallway, wearing an apron with a tea towel over her arm.

"Ah, there you are, Dak," she said, like it was her house not mine. "Mum looked a bit tired, so I'm making tea. I reckon you could both do with a good meal."

I bristled. She was *my* mum, not Mrs Baxter's and it was my job to look after her. I saw Mrs Baxter look at the carrier bag I was holding and I slid it behind my legs.

"Perhaps you'd like to help set the table," she suggested.

I frowned. "I'm going up to see my mum."

When I went into her bedroom Mum was standing on the bed, reaching up towards the ceiling.

"Mum, what are you doing?" I asked, bewildered.

"He's there," she moaned, her eyes fixed on the ceiling. "Can't you see his face?" She pointed upwards. "There, on the ceiling."

My heart sank and my stomach tightened. It was horrible seeing her like this. I didn't know what to say. I just stood, staring. After a few moments she let her arms fall to her sides and turned towards me.

"Dad's not there, is he?" she asked unhappily.

I shook my head. "You were just dreaming," I said. "I see him everywhere too." Which wasn't exactly true, but wasn't exactly a lie either. "Mrs Baxter's made tea," I added. I got Mum's dressing gown and helped her put it on, then we went downstairs together.

Mum sat in silence and hardly ate a mouthful of the macaroni cheese Mrs Baxter had prepared. I wanted to hug her, to take the hurt away. If only she knew the truth – then all this pain would drop away in an instant. I wanted to tell her, but I just didn't feel she was ready: "She's really quite ill," Doctor Doyle had said… What if my telling her made her worse?

But I might have been tempted if Mrs Baxter hadn't been there, which made me resent her even more – especially when she brought up the subject of school, suggesting it was about time I went back.

Mum looked at her as if struggling to recall who

I was, never mind whether I should return to school. "Well…" she murmured uncertainly.

"I'm not ready," I said firmly. "And, anyway, Mum needs me here."

"But the term's nearly over and you'll want to see your friends," Mrs Baxter persisted. "It would do you good, I'd have thought. I can look after Mum—"

"No, not yet," I insisted, cutting her off. "I'm not ready."

"Well, I think you should consider it," Mrs Baxter sighed. "You can't stay away for ever."

I opened my mouth to reply, then shut it again. I smiled, my irritation gone. Something about Mrs Baxter reminded me of a fish I'd seen that afternoon at the aquarium.

She looked like a giant pacu.

6

Mrs Baxter wasn't the only one who thought I should go back to school. When I picked up the post the next day, there was a letter from the school's admission office. It expressed sympathy, plenty of it, but also suggested strongly that a return to school before the end of term was "highly advisable for my well-being". Mr Hoskins, the headteacher, didn't want me to miss out on the end-of-year activities, the letter said. He thought they would be a good distraction for me.

The letter was friendly, but I sensed a note of ... well, not exactly threat, but demand in phrases such as "legal requirement". There was a mention of "counsellors" too. The meaning was clear: the school wanted me back and they expected Mum to go along with their wishes.

But I didn't want to go back to school. I didn't want to have to go through all the business of people saying how sorry they were and treating me differently, oddly. It made me shudder to think of it. It's why I'd avoided Ruby and Tom – and *they* were my best friends. I definitely didn't want to have to speak to a counsellor, to have a stranger poking about in my thoughts, asking me questions and trying to get me to talk about things I didn't want – or need – to talk about. I didn't want to sit in a classroom either and do Maths or English or watch films about World War II or go on a trip to some old castle or sailing ship. I didn't want life to go back to normal. I wanted to be free to go down to the aquarium each day, to talk to Dad and help look after the fish. Nothing was more important than that. I'd finished with school.

I thought about my options. I could simply throw the letter away – Mum wasn't reading her post anyway – but the way it was worded, it was obvious a response was expected: either my return to school or a convincing explanation for my absence. Correspondence between school and parents was normally by email. I knew Mum's email address and her password (I'd sent brief replies to the few messages of sympathy I'd found there after the funeral), so

I could easily reply to the admission office. But would that be enough? If I said that "Dak is still too upset and traumatized by what happened to return to school", would that satisfy them? No … I needed something more convincing.

The problem troubled me all day and spoilt my time down at the aquarium. I was so distracted that I upset Dad.

"What is the matter with you, son? I'd be better off trying to converse with a ray," he huffed and flounced off to his anemone.

Johnny noticed my distraction too. "You all right, mate?" he asked when I failed to respond to one of his instructions. I just wanted to get away and think.

Soon after I arrived home, Doctor Doyle came. Dad used to complain about how doctors never made home visits any more – but here she was visiting for the second time in just over a week.

She asked me how things were and I shrugged and said, "OK." It wasn't really true of course, but I didn't want her to think that Mum and I couldn't cope.

It was only when the doctor went upstairs that I noticed she'd left her large briefcase in the hallway.

I looked at it for a moment. Perhaps I should take it up to her? I slipped my hand through the handle of the case, but I didn't lift it. Instead I laid it flat on the ground and carefully flicked the catches.

The lid popped open on the expected collection of doctor's gear – a stethoscope, a thermometer, some wrapped syringes, a small torch, bottles of tablets, wipes... My heart leapt as I saw what I'd been hoping for underneath a bunch of blank prescription notes: a few sheets of headed notepaper. I took one, then quickly clicked the briefcase shut.

Later, when the doctor had gone and I'd settled Mum back in bed with a cup of tea and some toast (she wouldn't eat anything more – not even the chocolate I'd bought her), I sat at my desk to write the letter. I couldn't copy Doctor Doyle's writing because I didn't know what it looked like, but then no one at school would either, I reckoned. Everyone said that doctors' writing was terrible (it used to be a family joke that Dad should have been a doctor because his writing was so bad), so it wouldn't matter too much if the letter looked a bit scruffy – as long as it could be read, of course.

I took some time composing the letter on a piece of scrap paper, trying to make it sound convincing.

I liked writing and I was good at it. My English teacher often said how mature my writing was and what an impressive vocabulary I had (that was partly thanks to Dad, but also to Mum, who was a big reader – which had rubbed off on me). When we'd done persuasive writing at school, I'd got the top mark, but this was on another level. I wasn't just trying to get a good mark, I had to be believed. If I didn't get it right, I'd not only be in big trouble but my plans would be ruined. I'd have to go back to school and see a counsellor and…

Well, I had to get it right, that's all. For all our sakes, I had to.

But I couldn't do it. I took out the headed paper with Doctor Doyle's name on and stared at it. It was only a blank sheet of paper but it seemed suddenly as terrifying as a forest of demons. Each time I tried to start writing, my hand stiffened and I knew that I wouldn't be able to do it steadily and clearly. I banged my hand down on the desk. Why couldn't I do it? Why was I *so* weak?

7

I didn't sleep well. I wasn't someone who got into trouble. I didn't do bad stuff. My teachers liked me. But what would they say if they knew what I'd done?

In my dream Doctor Doyle caught me stealing the notepaper and loomed over me like a raging ogre. When I woke up, I was convinced for a moment or two that I really had been discovered... I reached under the pillow and felt the soft hump of Dad's sweatshirt, imagined its yellow smiley, and, slowly, I started to feel calmer.

I hadn't done anything too terrible, I told myself. It wasn't like I'd stolen the doctor's drugs or stethoscope – nobody was going to get hurt by what I'd done, were they? I decided to talk to Dad about what I was planning and see what he said. That made me feel a lot better. I wasn't on my own: Dad was still there. OK, he was a fish – but he was still Dad. He could give me advice – although, I had to admit, his advice wasn't always that great. Once when I was having trouble with a bigger boy at school, Dad told me to imagine him wearing a pink ballet dress with a wet fish on his head and then he wouldn't seem nearly as menacing. But it just made things worse because the next time I saw the boy I started grinning – and then he thumped me.

Still, maybe now Dad was a fish, things would be different; he'd be wiser, more dignified…

I wanted to go straight to the clownfish tank when I arrived at the aquarium, but Stephan stopped me.

"Ah, Dak," he said. "I was hoping to catch you before you left yesterday. "

"Sorry," I murmured. "I had to get back home. My mum needed me."

"Oh, of course. I understand." He smoothed his drooping moustache with a finger and thumb.

"Is there anything wrong?" I asked.

"No, no, not at all! It's just that there's someone I want you to meet."

I frowned. "Really? Who?" I asked warily. Meeting new people meant having to answer awkward questions.

"Well, come into the office and you'll see," Stephan said with a smile, which made me even more wary. I couldn't remember ever seeing Stephan smile. "Come on, then," he urged.

So I shrugged and followed him into the office.

The first thing that struck me was the mess. It was like the place had just been burgled. There were files, papers and books everywhere; some lay in untidy piles, but most were just strewn across the floor and the furniture – on the desk, a couple of tables, chairs, a battered metal filing cabinet. On the walls there were a few frayed fish posters, which had faded from sunlight and age. I might have been tempted to call the room a tip, if I hadn't known first-hand that the municipal rubbish tip (*Sorry, Dad, 'Recycling Centre'*) was in much better order than this.

The second thing that struck me was that there was someone in among the mess, sitting with their back to the door, hunched in front of a computer screen. It was to this person that Stephan now spoke.

"Violet," he said. "Violet, I've brought someone to meet you."

The response was a deep, theatrical sigh. Then slowly (as-if-to-make-a-point slowly) the person turned to face the room and I found myself gazing at the unsmiling features of a girl about my own age, possibly a little older. She had a long, pale face with dirty blonde hair, the colour of a dogfish's belly. She wore a grey, stripy T-shirt, blue denim shorts and white trainers. Her fingernails, still resting on the computer keyboard, were a vivid turquoise. Her eyes were on Stephan – she didn't look at me at all.

Stephan waved his large hand in my direction. "This is Dak," he said. Still the girl ignored me. She was either very shy or very rude, I thought. "Dak is our most dedicated customer. He comes to the aquarium every day. And now he's helping out with the feeding too."

The girl gave me a quick, hostile glance.

"Dak, this is my niece Violet," Stephan continued, "Violet McGee. Her school's broken up for the summer and her parents are away, so she's come to stay with me." He smiled again, but this time less confidently.

I thought I ought to say something. "Hi, Violet," I muttered.

Violet gave me an even more hostile glance. Her eyes were small, fierce and as startlingly bright green as a tree frog – and looked just as poisonous.

"Dak?" she snorted. "What sort of name is that?"

She frowned. "Can I go back to the computer now? I was in the middle of a game."

Very rude, I concluded.

Stephan apologized afterwards, but I was relieved. I just wanted to be with the fish. I'd already forgotten about Violet by the time I was in the murky tunnel that led to the main hall of the aquarium, with the reassuring sound of the water gurgling about me.

I saw Johnny standing on a table above a new fish tank he'd been setting up. He was testing the oxygen level with some sort of probe and then noting down the reading. The tank was alive with jellyfish. A light inside it made the jelly fish appear to change colour as they drifted through the water, pulsing like tiny umbrellas opening and shutting, streaming strands of what looked like lace as they floated up and down in a balletic dance. It was beautiful – mesmerizing.

"Amazing, ain't they?" said Johnny.

"Yes," I breathed. "Awesome."

"They can give ya a nasty sting though," he added. "Me mate's girlfriend was stung once out snorkling. He had to pee on her to take the pain away."

I pulled a face. "Is that really true?"

"Yeah, course it is. It's what ya have to do if a jelly-fish stings ya." Johnny jumped down off the table, his quiff bouncing and the crab tattoo on his neck twitching as he landed. "So – have ya met Violet?"

I nodded.

"Bit of a stinger herself, that one, eh?"

"She's not very friendly," I agreed.

"Ya can say that again." Johnny laughed. "She's pricklier than a lionfish."

He packed the probe away in its sheath. "Anyway, enough of her. We got fish to feed…"

8

I didn't get to talk to Dad until the afternoon. I helped Johnny with the feeding – and with some of the testing too.

Johnny showed me how to use the "optical probe" and check the reading on the unit. Then we tested the temperature of the tanks. These were all different depending on the fish and where they came from. The last tank we came to was Dad's. Clownfish were tropical so their tank needed to be warm – twenty-five degrees, Johnny said. He checked the temperature and it was fine.

"Well, what was that all about?" Dad asked when Johnny had gone off to put the equipment away.

I explained about the testing. "It *is* nice and warm in here," Dad conceded. "A bit like that hot tub in the hotel where we stayed on the Isle of Wight. Remember?" He grinned. "My swimming shorts kept filling up with water. I looked like I'd been inflated."

He wiggled with amusement. But I was feeling too nervous to react.

"You're not going all mute on me again, are you?" he said.

I shook my head. "No, Dad. It's just that I've got something I need to talk to you about."

"That sounds ominous," said Dad. "They're not moving me into the piranha tank, are they?"

"No, nothing like that," I assured him. A little hesitantly I told him about taking the notepaper from the doctor's case and about my plan to forge a letter to the school. Dad listened, his delicate fins rippling. "I tried to write the letter last night, but I couldn't. I felt so useless, like I was letting you and mum down."

I looked into the tank anxiously, waiting for Dad's reaction. Dad stared at me with his currant-black eyes and his lips seemed to form themselves into a smile.

"You're a good boy, Dak, and if I could I'd give you a pat on the back. Taking that piece of notepaper from the doctor's case was wrong – and you know it. That's why you couldn't write the letter. But you wanted to write it for the sake of your family – and nothing is more important than that. Life is about getting your priorities right – and that's what you're doing. School is important, of course it is. But right now, it can wait." He blew out a stream of bubbles. "Anyway you *are* coming to school, aren't you?" I frowned. "Aquariums are full of schools – schools of fish!" He wobbled with delight and I smiled with relief. Dad was on my side. "Now, got any food for me?"

"You've already been fed, Dad," I reminded him.

"Call those flakes food?" The clownfish snorted. "What's in them anyway?"

"They're called marine flakes." I said. "I don't know what they're made of."

"Well, do me a favour and try one of the other tubs next time, can you? The one that says Kentucky Fried Chicken flakes. That'd do nicely."

I laughed. "You really are a clown, Dad."

"What are you laughing at?" said a sharp voice behind me. I turned to see Violet scowling in the doorway. *How long has she been there?* I wondered anxiously. Had she overheard me talking with Dad?

"Oh, I – I—" I stammered. "The clownfish is … funny. The way it moves." I looked back at the tank. "It has a silly sort of wobble like it's trying to make you laugh."

Violet slouched over and stood next to me. She glared into the tank.

"Doesn't look funny to me. Just looks stupid. Fish are dumb."

"You only say that 'cos you don't know them."

"And you do?" Violet sneered. "What is there to know? They live underwater and swim around all day. Big deal."

"You're wrong," I insisted. "They're amazing."

"Really?" Violet snorted. "OK, tell me one 'amazing' thing about Nemo there."

"The clownfish?"

"Yeah, Nemo, the clownfish."

I took a deep breath. "Well, for a start he's not called Nemo."

"What is his name then?" Her voice was scratchy with hostility.

I was about to say "Bob", Dad's name, but stopped myself. It was my secret and I wasn't going to share it with anyone – least of all Violet. "He's a wild creature. He doesn't have a name. And I'll tell you something amazing about him." I pointed. "You see that thing he's resting in? It's called an anemone or a sea hedge-hog. Its tentacles are poisonous to all fish except the clownfish. Clownfish can settle on anemones and not get stung because their bodies are covered in a sort of sticky mucus that protects them."

Violet wrinkled her nose. "That's disgusting! You mean they cover themselves in slime?"

"Uh-huh," I nodded. I'd hooked her, I could see. Her eyes were less hostile.

"And I'll tell you something else," I went on. "They're hermaphrodites. They start off male but then they change into females."

Violet was obviously intrigued. "That's weird," she said. She thought for a moment, then smiled, revealing two vampire-like teeth at either side of her mouth. "Imagine if your dad suddenly turned into your mum." All at once her smile vanished. Her pale cheeks flushed. "Oh, sorry," she muttered. "I didn't mean... Stephan told me about your dad."

I shrugged. "It's OK."

Violet lifted her head again and the scowl was back. "Anyway, my dad's an arsehole. I wouldn't *care* if he was dead. I really wouldn't."

And she stormed away.

9

I didn't see Violet again before the aquarium shut, so I didn't find out what her dad had done to upset her so much. (Told her not to be so rude maybe?) Not that I really cared – I had enough stuff of my own to think about.

I went to the beach on my way home. The shingle sparkled blue and silver in the late afternoon sun. The tide was bustling in, the waves rushing over each other in a wild babble. A group of small kids were poking hopefully in the shallow rock pools at the water's edge, a shaggy black dog wagging its tail excitedly on the beach behind them.

I sat on an old groyne that had been softened by seaweed and gazed at the smooth but knobbly slabs of chalk in the shallows, among the green. Suddenly they seemed like grotesque, twisted white bodies and I quickly looked away.

Thoughts bubbled in my head, wild as the waves. So much had happened in the last twenty-four hours – and none of it good. Why couldn't everyone just leave me alone? Doctors, neighbours, head-teachers, angry girls... I didn't need any of them. All I wanted was to get on with my life, to look after Mum and see Dad at the aquarium each day. Was that too much to ask?

I picked up a pebble and hurled it at a cresting wave. I thought about Violet and hoped our paths wouldn't cross too often. Luckily for me she seemed much more interested in Stephan's computer than the fish and I'd be busy a lot of the time anyway help-ing Johnny. And Johnny didn't ask questions. All he was interested in was the fish, which suited me fine.

Back home, I decided to give Becks a change of hat. The straw boater was Dad's preferred summer hat for the bulldog, so I went to fetch that. The boater had come out of the rubbish so was a little battered, but Dad had done his best to restore it, even attaching a bright yellow ribbon round the crinkled rim. (I could hear him now singing as he did it, *Tie a yellow ribbon round the old straw hat…*) I swapped the Union Jack sun hat for the boater, perching it at an angle on the dog's head. The effect was ridiculous. Dad would have loved it.

Mum was in the sitting room and seemed a little more herself. OK, she was in her dressing gown not clothes, but she wasn't in bed or leaping at the ceiling, which had to be an improvement. She was staring at a picture. It was a photo of the three of us on a beach somewhere when I was little. The sand was very white and the sky a perfect azure.

"I've never seen that photo before," I said. "Where was it taken?"

"In France," Mum replied softly. "On the beach at Le Touquet. The sand dunes were amazing, like whipped ice-cream." She smiled sadly. "It was a perfect day."

"How old was I?"

Mum thought a moment. "You'd have been about two, I guess. You and your dad dug for hours in the sand." She stared at the photo again. "It was a perfect day," she repeated, struggling to hold back her tears. "I'm sorry, Dak. I want to be strong, I really do."

I put my arms around her. "It's all right, Mum." I hugged her tight until her sobbing stopped.

* * *

We ate a proper meal together, the first since Dad had gone. Mum made a cheese omelette and a salad (all from offerings left by Mrs Baxter). We sat and ate it in front of the TV. We started off watching a soap but Mum found it too upsetting, so I changed channels.

It was hard to find anything that wasn't upsetting in some way, but eventually we settled on a natural history programme about the Antarctic. The Emperor penguins made us both smile – Dad loved penguins and he used to imitate them, waddling and squawking to try to make me laugh when I was younger … especially if I was in a grump about something. It always worked.

Everything was going fine until the leopard seal arrived and started hunting the penguins. When it caught one, Mum couldn't watch any more.

"Sorry, love. I'm not feeling too good," she said shakily. "I'm going to go back to bed."

I switched off the TV. "Do you need anything?" I asked.

Mum shook her head. "No, thank you." She kissed me on the cheek. "I'll be all right. You carry on watching if you want."

I nodded, but I didn't turn the TV back on. I had a job to do. I went over and picked up the picture Mum had been looking at – the one taken on the beach in

France. If I'd been two, then the photo was nine years old. I hardly recognized myself. My hair was very blond, for a start, not mousy like it was now. My face was rounder too, chubby-cheeked. In the photo Dad had his arms around Mum and me and he was half grinning, half squinting in the bright sunlight. Apart from the fact that he was a bit thinner then and had more hair, he hadn't really changed much over the years. He looked out at me now, smiling, encouraging.

Go on, son, his expression seemed to say. *Do the right thing.*

I went up to my room, took out the headed note-paper and spread it out flat on my desk. Then I pulled Dad's sweatshirt out from under the pillow, held it against my face a moment or two and took a deep breath. I was doing this for my family, I told myself – and nothing was more important than that. Just like Dad had said. I had to look after Dad – and Mum – and I couldn't do that if I was in school all day. I put the sweatshirt down on the desk. It made me feel as if Dad was actually there, supporting me.

I practised writing the letter in a notebook, over and over, first in pencil, then in black biro. After a while I knew that I wasn't really practising any more, I was just putting off writing the real thing. I wished I'd taken more than one sheet of the notepaper in case I made any mistakes, but I hadn't so I'd just have to get it right first time. I laid the headed notepaper on top of a page of lined paper in my school topic exercise book.

I'd never written anything so carefully before. My hand felt tense but I tried to keep it steady; my tongue stuck out as it always did when I was concentrating really hard. It took me the best part of half an hour and when I'd finished, signing the doctor's name with a scratchy scrawl, my hands were clammy and shaky.

I cast my eyes over the letter one last time. Was it too neat? Did it look too childish? Would Mr Hoskins be fooled – or would he know it right away for the fake it was? I'd just have to keep my fingers crossed and hope for the best. I fetched an envelope and a stamp from the sitting-room desk, folded the letter neatly, pushed it into the envelope and sealed it shut. And sighed. It was done.

That night I dreamed of being a fish.

10

I posted the letter on my way to the aquarium, feeling better than I had for days. When I arrived, I found the doors locked. Peering through the glass, I could see that the reception area was full of decorating stuff: a ladder and paint pots and brushes. There were old sheets covering the floor. Stephan had his back to me, talking to a big man in white overalls.

I looked over to the reception desk and was surprised to see Violet staring out at me with what looked almost like a smile. She raised her hand as if to say "hi", then turned and said something to Stephan – who came over and unlocked the doors.

"We're shut this morning, Dak," he said. "I'm having some ornamentation done." I looked at him blankly. "Come in. I'll show you."

I hesitated. "I thought you said you were closed."

"To the general public, yes, but not to you."

As Stephan relocked the doors behind me, I looked around, puzzled. "But haven't these walls just been painted?" I said. I knew they had. Dad had remarked on it the last time he and I had come here together, just a month or so ago. He'd put his hand to his eyes and pretended to be dazzled by the shiny white walls.

"Painting was the first part of the plan," Stephan replied. "Today Toby here's going to carry out the second part."

Violet came over. "So what's he going to do, Uncle Stephan? Paint little fishes? Or maybe a giant shark?" She said it in a tone that made it clear she wasn't really interested. I wasn't sure if Stephan didn't get that she was being sarcastic or just chose to ignore it, but he responded as if her question was genuine. "No, Violet, he's not going to paint fish on the walls. He's going to paint *quotes* about fish."

"Quotes about fish?" I repeated, puzzled.

"Yes, quotations from famous people on the subject of fish," Stephan declared happily. "It'll give folks something to think about when they're walking around inside." I glanced at Violet and she rolled her eyes. Stephan reached into his jacket pocket and pulled out a piece of paper. He put on his reading glasses and, unfolding the paper, said, "Here's one from John Ruskin, the famous nineteenth-century art critic: *No human being, however great or powerful, was ever so free as a fish.*"

I smiled. "That's good," I said. "I like that." I thought of Dad, flitting about his tank, happy and carefree.

Violet shook her head. "But the fish here aren't free. Someone caught them, didn't they? And now they're imprisoned in this aquarium."

Stephan looked outraged. "This isn't a prison! It's a haven – for fish."

Violet snorted.

"Have you got any more quotes?" I asked quickly.

Stephan studied his sheet of paper thoughtfully, running his fingers over his droopy moustache. "This is one your dad liked, Dak. I showed it to him when I first had the idea of using quotes… It's by D. H. Lawrence: *To sink, and rise, and go to sleep with the waters…To be a fish!*"

"That's great!"

"Here's one: *Fish are best in batter with chips,*" Violet said. "That's a quote from Violet McGee."

Stephan frowned but wasn't put off. "This is *my* favourite: *I often sigh still for the dark downward and vegetating kingdom of the fish…*"

"That's creepy." Violet pouted.

For once I agreed with her. Something about it made me shiver. The words were beautiful but made me uncomfortable. "I prefer the other ones."

"I prefer mine," said Violet. "At least it makes sense."

11

Johnny had the morning off and there weren't any jobs for me to do. I wanted to go and have a chat with Dad, but Violet decided to attach herself to me. She wasn't nearly as grumpy as she'd been the day before – at least not to start with – but she still wasn't my idea of the perfect companion. She wasn't interested in fish for a start.

I showed her the lionfish with its amazing lacy flippers and deadly-poisonous spines. "What a stupid name – it doesn't look anything like a lion" was all she said. The golden pufferfish didn't fare any better ("Looks like he's swallowed a lemon"), or the longhorn cowfish ("Nothing should be allowed to be that ugly") or the glass catfish ("That's just freaky – why would you want to show off your insides?").

She wasn't impressed by facts either. I told her that

if starfish lose a leg they can grow another; that the Chinese softshell turtle can wee through its mouth; that a hagfish can fill a whole bucket with slime in a minute... She just screwed up her face and said it was gross.

The only time she showed any real interest was when we came to the piranha tank. "They look so mean," she said approvingly.

"You should see them at feeding time," I told her. "They go crazy. The food's gone in seconds. Sometimes they go so crazy they bite each other. That's why some of them, like that one there—" I pointed— "have got a bit of their tail missing."

Violet stared into the tank in dark fascination. "I bet they'd rip us to shreds if we fell in there." Her tone was of admiration rather than fear. "Some beetles are like that. They can strip a carcass in no time at all."

"Are you interested in beetles?" I asked, surprised.

"My stupid dad is," Violet scowled. "He's obsessed with them. That's why I'm here. He's gone on one of his trips to Africa to study some rare beetle and my mum went with him." Her scowl deepened. "They wouldn't let me go."

"Is that why you're so angry with your dad?" I said. "It's not that terrible."

Violet glowered at me. "You don't know anything about it! I told you, my dad's an arsehole. He doesn't live with us any more – he split up with my mum."

I was confused. "But they've gone to Africa together?"

"Don't remind me!" Violet snapped. She waved her hand angrily in a flash of turquoise. "He can't make up his mind, can he? He thinks maybe he'd like to come back."

"Wouldn't that be a good thing?" I suggested hesitantly.

Violet's cheeks flushed as if they were about to catch fire. "I wish he would just leave us alone." She sighed deeply. "Look, I'm sorry about your dad, Dak, I really am. But if he was anything like mine, then you're better off without him. Dads just mess up your life."

I didn't know what to say. There didn't seem to be anything I *could* say that wouldn't just upset Violet more, so I shut up and looked at the fish.

Violet's bluntness didn't bother me. It was actually quite refreshing. No matter what she said, she couldn't upset me. She didn't know what I knew. She didn't know Dad was here, a clownfish. She wasn't interested in my life – she was only really interested in herself. And that meant she wouldn't ask me awkward questions.

* * *

I went down to the beach on my way home and looked out over the sea to the horizon. The water was flat and green and there was not a boat to be seen. Everything was so still and calm. If I closed my eyes I could feel myself disappear, become almost nothing – like a grain of sand.

Almost. But not quite. A worrying thought popped into my head: what if the Head, Mr Hoskins, read my letter and decided to ring Mum to see if there was anything he could do to help. He might do that, he was a nice man – and the thought made me panic for a moment or two. But then I remembered that Mum never answered the phone these days. She let it go to answer phone and asked me to check it in case there was anything urgent. If Mr Hoskins did ring, his message would end up there.

There was nothing to worry about. It was all going to be OK.

12

I was a little later than usual arriving at the aquarium the next morning and I found Johnny talking with Violet.

"Violet's been asking me about the fish," he said.

I frowned at Violet. "Really? I thought you thought fish were dumb."

"True," Johnny agreed. "I didn't figure you for a fish lover, Violet."

"I'm not," Violet replied brusquely. "But I've got to do something to pass the time. And Dak seems to think they're 'fascinating'."

"They are," Johnny confirmed with a nod of his black quiff. "They're the most fascinating creatures in the world. Ain't that so, Dak?"

"Definitely," I agreed.

He doesn't know the half of it, I thought to myself.

Johnny offered to take us on a behind-the-scenes tour of the aquarium. We started off in a room full of machines with buttons and pipes and dials that Johnny called the "engine room".

"How much water do ya reckon flows into this aquarium from the sea every day?" he quizzed us.

"I've no idea," said Violet in a tone that suggested she didn't much care either.

"Nor me." I shrugged.

"A hundred thousand litres!" Johnny exclaimed, throwing his arms out wide. "And we have to manage it and make sure it's right for all the different fish we've got here."

I knew that a hundred thousand litres was a lot but I couldn't imagine it. Would it fill a large swimming pool – or two? A football stadium?

Johnny moved on, pointing out various pumps and filters: the sand filter, the mechanical filter, which got rid of dirt, and the biological filter – "To make bacteria," he explained. "People think bacteria's a bad thing, but it ain't. We all need bacteria – the right kind, that is – to survive."

Violet looked less than convinced.

Next Johnny introduced us to the foam fractionator,

an impressive-looking device with a large cylindrical body topped by a transparent drum. Its job was to skim off protein. Protein was bad apparently, as were ammonia and nitrites – though ni*trates*, in small levels, were fine.

Science wasn't my best subject at school and I was lost by this point. Violet nodded, as if she were taking it all in and understood perfectly, but when Johnny's back was turned she crossed her eyes and grinned at me.

Johnny was talking about the importance of controlling the tanks' oxygen levels and temperature, which I knew about from working with him – but then he went on to PH and salinity and I was lost again. It was all too complicated. There was so much machinery and science needed to keep the fish healthy and alive.

"What happens if there's a power cut? How would the fish survive?" I asked. *Could they survive?*

Johnny smiled and pointed to another row of machines. "Emergency generators. If the tanks fail, these fellas will supply all the power that's needed."

The next stop was the feeding bay, where the food for all the different fish was prepared and stored – the large tubs of flakes that Dad was so sniffy about, as well as piles of chopped vegetables.

Of course it was the piranhas' diet that interested

Violet. "They eat a mixture of fresh fruit and veg, and meat and fish," Johnny told her.

"What sort of meat and fish?" Violet wanted to know.

"Trout, mice, chicks," said Johnny. "They ain't fussy."

"Mice? Chicks? That's gross!" Violet sounded horrified, but I could see again the dark fascination in her eyes. What *was* it with her and piranhas?

The last stop on the tour was the breeding area. We looked in a tank of black and white Banggai cardinals.

"Dad looks after the eggs," Johnny declared, nodding at the next tanks. "Same as with the seahorses. Those babies are just a few days old. They hatched out of a pouch in their dad's stomach." Violet and I stared in.

The seahorse babies were tiny, hardly more than dark flakes in the water, but they were already perfectly formed.

"They've got more chance of surviving here than if we was to leave them in their normal tank," said Johnny sombrely. "Baby seahorses ain't very strong. Even a slight change in temperature can kill them. In the wild only about one in a thousand survives."

"One in a thousand!" Violet was shocked.

I shivered.

"The dads look after the eggs and push them out when it's time," Johnny explained. "After that the babies have got to fend for themselves."

Violet tossed her head. "That's dads for you. They do half the job, then walk away."

Johnny disagreed. "It's just nature. Ya can't blame the dads."

"Violet can. She thinks dads are to blame for everything," I said.

"They are," Violet insisted. "They're a waste of space."

Johnny frowned. "Steady," he said, looking at me with concern.

"It's OK," I said. "My dad's not like that."

I smiled to myself. My dad was amazing. He was the funniest, kindest, most loving, best dad ever. My dad, the clownfish.

When I got home the phone was flashing red – which meant there was a message. Anxiously I pressed the button: Mr Hoskins had received the doctor's letter and was phoning to discuss it. He wanted Mum to call him back...

I quickly pressed delete, but I couldn't delete the

problem. I could just ignore the message and not tell Mum. But he'd just ring back another day and if he got no reply again, then what? I knew the answer and it made me feel sick: he'd send someone round. I was sure of it. Then I'd really be in trouble, but worse, all my plans would be ruined. I'd have to go back to school.

The thought made me hot and panicky. My breath seemed to get trapped in my chest and wouldn't come out. I felt weak and helpless, like one of those tiny baby seahorses. I had to go outside and sit in the porch with my head between my knees, taking deep breaths to calm myself. Maybe Mr Hoskins would understand if I explained…?

But even as my hopes rose they popped like bubble-gum. To make him understand I'd have to explain about Dad, and no grown-up – especially not a head-teacher – was going to accept that my father was a fish.

13

I went to see Dad as soon as I arrived at the aquarium next morning. I'd slept badly and not even his sweat-shirt could soothe me. I needed to see him, be with him.

He was swimming from one side of the tank to the other, so fast that he seemed to shimmer through the water. I watched him mesmerised. After about the fourth turn I called out to get his attention.

"What is it? Can't you see I'm busy?" he hissed.

"I just came to say 'hello'," I said meekly.

"Well, now you've said it. Can I please get back to my practice?"

"Practice?" I frowned. "What are you practising for?"

Dad wiggled to the front of the tank. "The damsels have challenged me to a race," he announced dramat-ically. "Fifty widths."

"When?"

"When I'm ready. I'm not racing till I'm sure I'll win."

"But how can you ever know that?"

"*Fin*tuition, my boy," Dad said with a wink. "Do you remember the octopus that predicted all the World Cup results? Paul, I think his name was. Well, he'll look like an amateur next to me." He flickered with pride. "Those damsels are going to be in distress all right. And no one's going to rescue them. Clownfish rule OK!"

Then he was off again, swimming from side to side.

Upstairs, Toby had finished his painting – the walls were covered with fish quotes in his graceful script. Over the reception desk was the creepy one that had made me shiver: *I often sigh still for the dark downward and vegetating kingdom of the fish.* The name Robert Lowell was written underneath. Who was he, I wondered? An ecologist, a writer, a poet…? I preferred the other quotes – but, I had to admit, this one suited Stephan best.

I looked to see if he was in his office, but he wasn't. Violet was. She was on the floor by the desk.

"Hi, Violet," I said. She didn't look up. "What are you doing?"

"I'm trying to put this place in order," she growled, staring at a mess of papers.

"Oh."

Violet sat up. "Is that all you can say: 'Oh'?"

"I mean, it's a big job," I offered lamely.

She nodded. "It is." She gave me an almost-smile and her eyes were almost friendly. "Fancy helping?"

I shrugged. "OK."

I'd rather have been with the fish, but right now any distraction would do.

We worked hard, tidying and sorting. Violet made new files and put them neatly in the cabinet. She didn't say a lot and nor did I. Now and then I asked her where things should go and let her decide. She didn't know the office any better than I did really but there was an air of confidence about everything she did.

"You don't say much, do you, Dak?" Violet remarked after we'd been working for some time. I started to shrug but she went on with a smile, "Unless it's about fish."

I tried to smile back but there was too much going on in my head.

"Dak's a strange name," she said, but not in a sneering way like when we were first introduced.

"Violet's not exactly common," I replied defensively.

"No, but it is a name." She paused a moment as if

collecting her thoughts. "What I mean is, I've never heard the name Dak before. Did your parents make it up?"

"My dad did. My mum wanted to call me Zak. But Dad thought it was too ordinary. Like his name: Bob. He wanted me to have an unusual name."

"So Zak became Dak?"

"Yes."

"But is it short for something, like Zak's short for Zachary?"

I shook my head. "No. Although when I was little Dad used to say it was short for pterodactyl."

"Pterodactyl!"

"It was a joke." I smiled, but again without conviction.

"You look like you're worried about something," Violet said.

Her sudden change of subject took me by surprise. "Me? Uh…"

"Is it something to do with your dad?"

"No, no, it's… Well…"

"Tell me," she ordered, her bright green eyes staring at me.

And, well, why not? I thought. So I did. Not about Dad being a clownfish, of course, but I told her about the letter I'd written and the headteacher's phone call and my worry that I'd be found out and have to go back to school.

In the few days I'd known her, Violet had already surprised me several times. But now her reaction astonished me.

"Oh, is that all?" she said casually. "I can fix that."

14

I didn't get Violet's solution at first.

"I'm good at acting," she said. "I go to drama club. Last term I played Mary Poppins and had excellent reviews."

I stared at her. "What's Mary Poppins got to do with my problem?"

"*Mary Poppins* hasn't got anything to do with it," Violet huffed. "It's just an example. To show you I'm good at acting and can play different characters, see?"

"No, not really," I said. Violet rolled her eyes and sighed like I was being really, really stupid.

"Look, sometimes, on the phone, I pretend to be my mum. No one ever guesses it's me. I fool people all the time."

"Ah, I get it … I think," I said hesitantly. "You're going to pretend to be my mum?"

"Exactamento!" Violet whooped. "I'll phone your school and talk to your headmaster. Problem solved."

She made it all sound so simple, but I knew it wasn't. "What if he doesn't believe you?"

This possibility didn't seem to have occurred to Violet and she fell silent for a moment. "I'll speak through a handkerchief," she said at last. "It makes your voice sound different. They do it in films all the time."

"Does that really work? Won't you just sound odd?" I said doubtfully. Another problem struck me. "Have you even got a handkerchief? I haven't."

As it happened, Violet hadn't either but she looked around for something that she could use instead. The best she could do was the sleeve of her hoodie, but that didn't work – you couldn't hear a word she was saying.

"It's no good," I said.

Violet frowned, then asked, "How well does the head know your mum? Have they spoken much before?"

I shook my head. "Maybe once or twice. Not for a while."

Violet's eyes gleamed. "Perfectissimo! Then we've nothing to worry about!"

"Really? But what will you say?"

"What do you want me to say?"

I thought about this. "I want you to say that you think I should stay at home and not go back until after the summer holidays."

"Why?"

"Why what?"

"Why do I think you should stay at home?"

I frowned. "You know. Because of … because…"

"Because your dad died and you're still in shock."

"Yes." I shuffled some papers on the desk. Facing Violet was almost as bad as facing Mr Hoskins.

"And what do I say if he wants to come round?"

I shuddered. "He can't. He mustn't."

"It's all right, Dak." Violet's face lit up. She was really enjoying herself now. "I'll tell him the doctor's said you have to have rest and quiet. People always follow doctors' orders." She grinned. "I think *I'll* be a doctor one day."

I was a bit worried that Violet would say the wrong things, so we had a rehearsal. She pretended to be Mum and I pretended to be Mr Hoskins. It went fine until I asked her a question and she told me to stop being so nosy.

"I don't think you should say that," I told her.

"With respect, Mr Hoskins, Dak is my son and I think I know what's best for him," Violet fired back.

I shook my head. "I wasn't being Mr Hoskins then; I was being me. *I* don't think you should say that."

"Oh," said Violet. Then she started to giggle and soon I was giggling too. When we'd finally calmed down, I said, "What if you start laughing while you're talking to Mr Hoskins?"

"I won't," Violet assured me. "I told you, I'm good at this. *Very* good."

I used the office computer to look up the school telephone number. Then I locked the door in case Stephan appeared suddenly and ruined everything. Violet said she'd put the phone on speaker so I could listen in and help out if there were any tricky questions she couldn't answer.

"Here we go... Wish me luck," she said brightly.

"Good luck," I croaked.

"No, you have to say, 'Break a leg'. That's what they say in the theatre."

"OK. Break a leg." *But how can you act if your leg's broken?* I thought. Then I heard the ring tone and felt my stomach drop down to my shoes.

"Good morning, Middlemas School," the school

secretary, Mrs Burns, chirruped from the speaker.

Violet gave me a wink. "Good morning, this is Mrs Marsden, Dak's mum. I'm returning Mr Hoskins' call." Her voice was deeper, calmer. It was amazing how different she sounded. "Could I have a word with him, please?"

I cringed, waiting for Mrs Burns to laugh or make some sharp remark that showed she hadn't been fooled – but she just said, "I'll put you through, Mrs Marsden. And may I offer my condolences. We were all really really sorry to hear of your loss."

"Thank you," Violet replied with quiet dignity. Then she turned to me with a broad grin.

We waited a moment or two and then, "Good morning, Mrs Marsden." Mr Hoskins was on the line!

There was no doubt about it – Violet was a "phenomenon". That was the word Dad used when he was talking about someone who had extraordinary talent, like a footballer: *That guy's a phenomenon*, he'd say.

Well, so was Violet. Not once did Mr Hoskins sound suspicious – he was very concerned when Violet had told him how shocked and upset I still was by Dad's death, and how the doctor had advised her that I should have more time to recover before going back to school. The only tricky moment came when he suggested sending someone round with some books and papers so that I could see what the class had been up to while I'd been away. I shook my head wildly. Violet gestured that she needed my help, but my mind went blank with panic.

Just when I thought everything was ruined, Violet said, "I think Dak and I may go away for a while to help him take his mind off things. A stay in the country perhaps…"

"Oh, yes, of course, I understand," Mr Hoskins said at once. "That sounds like a very good idea."

"Perhaps you could send some work through by email," Violet added brightly.

Mr Hoskins liked this idea. He said he'd tell my form tutor to get in touch. And that was it: problem solved. When Violet put down the phone we high-fived and whooped. Violet had fixed it just as she'd said she would. She was a phenomenon. Prickly, bossy, moody, rude – but definitely a phenomenon.

15

Over the next few days Violet and I spent a lot more time together – and I actually enjoyed being with her. She could still have her scratchy moments, but all in all she was much more easy-going than when she'd first arrived. She really got involved with the aquarium too.

One morning I came in to find her in charge of the reception desk. She was filing her nails, which seemed brighter than ever.

"Uncle Stephan's busy showing a couple of men around," she explained.

"A couple of men?"

"Yes, from the council. Health and Safety. Apparently they do random checks now and then. Like those busybody inspectors you get in school."

"Ofsted," I nodded. "We had them at the beginning of the summer term."

"We had them last year," said Violet. She grimaced. "The teachers went mental. Every wall in the school had a display on it. It was like they were trying to turn the place into an art gallery. A really rubbish art gallery."

"Mr Hoskins said we should act like normal," I said.

"Our head wouldn't dare say that," Violet replied. "The school would be shut down immediately." She sighed and shook her head. "Our school's full of lunatics."

A customer came in, a woman with a small child in a pushchair, and Violet took her money and gave her a ticket. She did it all so easily, as if she'd been sorting out tickets all her life – I'd have been in a total muddle, I was sure.

While I waited for Violet, I glanced idly around the foyer. I thought about the two men from the council. What were they here to inspect, I wondered? Was it the health and safety of the *fish* that they were concerned about, or the people who visited? The aquarium wasn't dangerous … unless of course you got into the lionfish tank or tried to swim with the stingrays. Then you'd be in trouble. Violet would no doubt add the piranhas to the list of perils but actually piranhas don't really attack humans, Johnny told me. It's just a myth.

A couple more customers came in, keeping Violet busy a while longer. My thoughts wandered back to our inspection: Mr Hoskins telling us all to be ourselves and that everyone was an ambassador for the school. *I'm very proud of you*, he'd said. *I know you'll treat our visitors with politeness and respect."* And we had, too. The school had been classed "outstanding" and Mr Hoskins had thanked everyone when the inspectors had gone.

There had been a special atmosphere in the school those few days: a feeling of togetherness, of excitement, of happiness. For an instant it all came back to me, but as if through deep water: the din of the playground, the clatter of the canteen, my form tutor's voice, Scottish, husky, Ruby's funny giggle, Tom's crazy wolf-whistle, the bell ringing for the end of break...

Another life. Someone else's life. Before...

"My mum Skyped me last night," Violet said, when she'd sorted her stream of customers. "Apparently she and my dad are having a wonderful time."

"That's good," I said carefully.

"Yeah, marvellous … for *them*. Mum hardly asked me a thing about how I'm doing. She was too busy gushing about how lovely the place was where they're staying and all the fascinating people they've met – and the amazing wildlife. Then my dad came on – and what do you think he talked about?"

"I don't know."

"Beetles! I wanted to slap his glasses off."

I couldn't help smiling. But Violet wasn't amused.

"What are you grinning about?" she hissed.

The answer came without me having to think. "My dad wore glasses," I said simply. "Well, sort of."

"What do you mean 'sort of'?" Violet managed to sound irritated and intrigued at the same time. "Like, he wore them for reading and stuff? Lots of people do that."

"No, he didn't wear them for reading. He wore them for work."

"What, at the rubbish dump? Why would you need glasses for that?"

I shook my head. "He didn't *need* glasses. His eyesight was fine. He wore them because he thought it made him look dignified – that people would respect him more if he wore glasses. He never wore them at home."

Violet gave me a pitying look. "I know you think your dad was the most amazing person in the world ever, Dak, but you've got to admit he was weird."

Was Dad weird? No… A bit crazy at times perhaps, but all the better for that. What would Violet say if she knew the truth? I wondered.

I reminded Dad about the glasses when I visited him later. Like so many things in the house, they'd started off as rubbish. "You found a box of frames at work, remember?" He'd brought the frames back one evening and shown them to me and Mum. There were several pairs – eight or nine at least – in a shoebox. He picked out a sturdy tortoiseshell pair and tried them on.

Well, how do I look? he'd asked, arms spread wide, beaming.

You look ridiculous, Bob, Mum had said, but not unkindly.

You look mad, Dad. I'd laughed.

That was when he'd first mentioned his idea about wearing glasses to get respect. *People look at you like you're dirt, because you work at the rubbish dump*, he said. *Except for Charlie. Everybody's always nice and polite to Charlie. And do you know why? Because he wears glasses. He looks intelligent. He looks dignified.*

He'd pushed the frames further up his nose. *Well, from now on I'm going to wear glasses too.*

"Why are you talking to me about glasses?" said the clownfish. "I'm a fish. What would I want with glasses?" He wriggled and pouted. "Unless I wanted to make a spectacle of myself. Get it? Make a *spectacle* of myself!"

A giggle of bubbles gushed from his mouth. Yes, my dad was a *clown*fish all right.

16

After helping Johnny with the feeding that afternoon, I went up to the foyer to look for Violet. I found Stephan leaning against the desk with his chin on his hands, his face as droopy as his long moustache. He looked as if the thing that Dad used to say may never happen finally had.

"What's up?" I asked. "Is something wrong?"

Stephan sighed deeply. It was the sigh of a man who'd spent too long in the dark downward and vegetating kingdom of the fish. "It's a disaster. A total catastrophe."

"What is?"

"Those men I showed around today…"

"Health and Safety – Violet told me."

"Health and Safety?" Stephan grumbled. "They're

hatchet men, sent by the council to ruin me."

"To ruin you? I don't understand. What's happened?"

Violet appeared from the office with a face like an angry piranha. "I'll tell you what's happened," she growled. "Those stupid men are trying to close down the aquarium."

Stephan said he'd known for days that the inspectors were coming but he thought it would be no more than a routine visit. They might make comments about a few minor issues, but nothing more.

"But one of the inspectors was from the building department and he kept asking questions about maintenance levels and how often I had checks carried out on the condition of the walls and roof and whether I'd had any work done recently that he ought to know about… It was like I had the place on the market and he was a potential buyer."

"And then he found something," Violet muttered venomously.

"What?" I asked.

"A problem with one of the walls," said Stephan. "The one on the sea side in the main hall. Apparently there's damp and the structure's unsound. It's got to be repaired – maybe even replaced. They've given me a fortnight to get the work started or they'll declare the aquarium unsafe and I'll have to close."

"Oh," I said. I felt oddly relieved. I'd feared worse. People had walls rebuilt all the time. Our next-door neighbours had had a problem with damp in their wall, and some builders had put up scaffolding and bashed and chipped away – and made the necessary repairs – and after a week or two everything had been fine. "That's not so bad, is it?"

Stephan goggled at me as if I'd told him water wasn't wet. "Not bad?! It's a disaster, a catastrophe. Those kinds of repairs cost thousands – maybe *tens* of thousands." His face sagged. "I don't have that sort of money, Dak."

"But you could borrow it, couldn't you, Uncle Stephan?" Violet said. "My dad's always borrowing money from the bank for his silly expeditions. I'm sure they'd lend you some to save the aquarium."

Stephan sighed so deeply he seemed to actually deflate. "I already owe the bank a great deal of money. I'm right at the limit. I can't borrow any more. If they insist on these repairs, I'll have no choice: I'll have to close the aquarium. I'll have to sell the place."

I could feel my chest tighten. I felt suddenly hot with panic.

"You can't think like that, Uncle Stephan; maybe the

repairs won't be as major or expensive as you think." Violet was trying to sound reassuring but I could hear the worry in her voice.

I couldn't breathe. I had to get outside into the fresh air. I ran across the foyer, pushed open the glass doors and stumbled out into the warm afternoon. I gasped and sucked in air in short shaky gulps. Violet had followed me. "Are you all right, Dak?"

I still had no breath to speak. *Close the aquarium! Close the aquarium! Close the aquarium!* echoed round and round in my head.

Violet put her hands on my shoulders and held them hard. "Slow down, breathe deeply," she instructed.

I tried to do as I was told, gradually taking in more air. My gulps grew deeper and steadier. I felt cooler and the tightness in my chest loosened.

"Phew," Violet muttered. "You had me worried there." Her thin, bony face was paler than ever. "I know you love this place, Dak, and you'd hate to see it close, but it's not life and death we're talking about."

I dropped my head again, shut my eyes. *But it is*, I thought. *That's exactly what it is.*

17

The next day a builder came in. He agreed with the Health and Safety inspectors: the wall was in bad shape. It was letting in water and needed a lot of repairs. It should really be replaced, but at the very least it needed repointing and plastering.

Stephan reported all of this with gloomy resignation to Violet and me and we listened in equally gloomy silence. There didn't seem to be anything to say – nothing constructive anyway.

The following morning Stephan received the builder's written report along with his quotation for carrying out the necessary work.

"Ten thousand pounds!" he groaned. "Where am I going to find ten thousand pounds?"

Violet and I looked at him helplessly. It was like there had been a power cut and the emergency generators hadn't kicked in. There was nothing we could do.

The mood of gloom affected Johnny too. He wasn't his normal self that afternoon when we were feeding the bass. Even his quiff seemed less bouncy than usual.

"Poor fish," he muttered. "Who knows what's gonna happen to them if we have to shut down the aquarium." He shook his head grimly. "It's a tragedy."

I felt my stomach lurch. "It mustn't happen. We can't let it."

"There ain't much we can do to stop it," Johnny replied. "We need a blooming miracle."

A miracle? I thought. Well, miracles did happen. Wasn't Dad turning into a clownfish a kind of miracle? Weren't those baby seahorses surviving in the breeding tanks a miracle? We just needed one more. Though right now it was hard to see where it was going to come from...

When I visited Dad, I didn't mention the aquarium's problems. Usually I liked to tell him my worries, but there was nothing he could do about this – and it would only upset him.

"How's tricks?" I asked, copying one of his own special phrases.

Dad flapped his little fins vigorously. "Tricks, tricks? I'm not a flippin' seal, you know."

"You are a clown, though," I reminded him. "You're always joking around."

His little mouth opened and shut in an unamused pout.

"Come on, tell me a joke," I prompted. "And not that one about rays and flounders."

Dad gave a pleased little wiggle. "OK, here's one for you. What do you call a deaf piranha?"

"I don't know, what *do* you call a deaf piranha?"

"Anything you like, 'cos he can't hear you."

I smiled weakly.

Dad tried another one. "What's a sea monster's favourite meal?"

"I don't know, Dad, what *is* a sea monster's favourite meal?"

"Fish and ships." The clownfish quivered with laughter. "Get it? Fish and ships!"

"Yes, I get it." I shrugged. "It's just not that funny."

"Not that funny? Not that funny?! How can you say it's not funny?"

Now I'd upset Dad – and I'd so wanted not to.

"Well, it's a bit funny," I conceded. "Maybe I'm just not in the mood."

I knew I'd made the right decision not to tell him about the problem with the aquarium wall. He didn't want to hear difficult stuff. He never had when he was a man – so why would he now that he was a fish?

I searched for something cheerful to say. "Mum seems to be getting better."

"Oh … good," said the clownfish vaguely. "What's the matter with her?

"Dad!" I exclaimed. "She's been missing *you*, of course. She thinks you're dead."

Dad darted away then suddenly swished back. "You mean you haven't told her that I'm … a fish?"

I shook my head.

"Don't you think it's time you did?"

"I didn't think she was ready. She's been really ill, Dad."

"Oh." His head wobbled. "Well, there's not much I can do, is there, in here?" His black beady eyes seemed without expression. "Well, send her my love – and look after yourself."

Then he turned again and swam away. I opened my mouth to say, "Goodbye," but closed it again when I heard footsteps clacking on the stone floor behind me.

I turned to see Johnny there, frowning. "I thought I heard voices," he said.

I tensed. Then forced a smile. "It was just me, talking to the fish."

"I reckon you'll get a lot more sense out of them than those muppets from the council," Johnny muttered darkly. Then with a shake of his quiff, he walked away.

I breathed deeply, relieved. My secret was still safe.

18

Mum was up and dressed when I got home. She'd even brushed her hair and put on a little make-up. She hadn't done that for ages. I was pleased to see her looking so much better – but it was hard, too, because she kept asking me questions about the aquarium and I really didn't want to talk about that.

My head was whirring. I just wanted to be on my own to think. If the aquarium had to be sold or shut down, what would happen to the fish? What would happen to Dad? Where would he go? He might be transferred to some other aquarium miles and miles away, somewhere where I wouldn't be able to visit. He'd be really miserable and lonely… I pictured him swimming round and round with no one to talk to, nobody to laugh at his jokes…

I felt sick with anxiety. Everything been looking up until the inspection. Now it all seemed to be falling apart.

I was glad when Mum suggested that I go to the chip shop to get dinner. She also suggested we share a piece of cod but I told her that now I spent so much time at the aquarium I couldn't eat fish any more.

I didn't tell her the main reason: that Dad – her husband – *was* a fish. I couldn't, no matter what Dad said. I still didn't feel the time was right.

It was a relief to get out of the house but my thoughts were all over the place. I felt weighed down with the secrets I was carrying. I was already keeping a huge secret from Mum and now I was keeping one from Dad too. I was doing it to protect them both – like I was the parent and they were the children, but I didn't know how much longer I could keep it up.

I passed Mrs Baxter in the street, but didn't stop. The last thing I wanted right now was to face her. She called out to me, but I put my head down and kept walking.

When I got to the chip shop I couldn't go in. From the doorway I saw the coated fish behind the glass of the hot cabinet, battered and eyeless. The heat and the smell of fat frying was too much and I had to turn away quickly into the open air.

I leant against the shop's window sweating, gasping, feeling like I was going to be sick. Sinking down until I was sitting on the pavement with my head bent forward, I tried to take deep breaths like Violet had told me.

"Dak?" I didn't respond at first because I thought the voice was inside my head. "Dak?" The voice was louder now and turquoise-nailed fingers reached for my shoulder.

This time I knew it was real. I looked up blurrily. "Violet," I croaked.

"Are you all right, Dak?" she asked. Her concern didn't last long. "You look like a tramp down there."

I smiled weakly. "I felt a bit faint. But I'm better now."

"You'd better get up then. You're blocking the pavement."

"Yeah, sorry." I pushed myself up. Violet was staring at me, waiting for an explanation. "I came to get some sausages and chips. But I suddenly felt faint and couldn't go in."

Violet looked confused. "You are strange, Dak. You cope really well with something huge like your dad dying, but you freak out about going into a fish and chip shop."

I shrugged. "I suppose I'm just worried about the aquarium."

"You worry too much," Violet said. Then she smiled broadly. "Anyway, I've got a plan."

Violet went into the chip shop and got my order. Then she she told me about her plan as we walked along together. It was simple, she said. We'd start a campaign to save the aquarium.

"We'll get up a petition, and contact the press, and maybe even raise funds."

"What, you and me?"

"Exactamento! We'll get Uncle Stephan and Johnny involved too, of course, but we'll do most of the work. What do you think? Brilliant, eh?"

I wasn't quite sure what to think. Only hours before Violet had seemed as depressed and defeated as me, but now she was back to her sparky, decisive self: Violet, the phenomenon.

"My dad does stuff like this all the time," she went on confidently. "He's involved with loads of campaigns to save beetles and termites and creepy-crawly creatures that you and I have never heard of but are essential to the world's eco-system *apparently*. You just have to make people believe that what you're campaigning for is amazing and indispensable."

I looked at her doubtfully. "*I* believe that. But you don't. You don't really like fish."

Violet frowned. "That's not the point. It's the principle. People who *are* interested in fish should have the right to see them in the aquarium. Imagine what a fuss there would be if the local football stadium was shut down."

I still wasn't convinced. "Lots of people care about football. I don't know how many really care about fish."

"Then we'll make them care! We'll make them see what a vital place the aquarium is – not just for entertainment, but for ecology and learning and making the world a better place." She paused with her arm outstretched dramatically, then broke into a grin. I grinned back: her enthusiasm was impossible to resist.

"So, are you with me?" she demanded, raising her right hand.

"Yeah. I'm with you." I raised my own hand and we high-fived.

19

At lunchtime the next day Violet and I went down to the beach. She said we'd think better if we were away from the aquarium, and I agreed. We found an opening low down in the cliff face, away from the crowds, and sat with our legs dangling, looking out at the departing tide. The hazy sun was like a lazer on the water, cutting the sea into two.

A small dark spider crawled lightly over Violet's hand and she lifted it up to take a closer look. "I love spiders," she said. "I love the way they move, the webs they weave, how they trap and kill their prey." Her eyes gleamed with pleasure. "Did you know all spiders, except one, are venomous?"

"No... I thought it was just tarantulas and black widows – and scary spiders like that."

Violet looked smug. "Most people do. Spiders use the venom to paralyse their victims. It's in their fangs." She opened her mouth in a weird snarl. "I've got fangs, too – see?"

I'd noticed them before: two small, sharp-looking teeth at either side of her mouth. "My dad used to say I was a vampire." She smiled, almost affectionately.

"So you didn't always hate him then."

"He wasn't always an arsehole."

She'd bought a cheeseburger on the way to the beach and she started to unwrap it.

"We can share it," she said.

I shook my head. "You have it. I'm not hungry."

"Suit yourself." She took a bite and munched.

Sometimes, after we'd visited the aquarium on a Saturday, Dad would take me for a burger as a treat. He made out it was a treat for me, but I knew it was more for him really. He loved burgers. He'd started to get a bit of a belly in the last year or so before he … transformed. Mum said he needed to start eating more healthily, to cut out the burgers and the fry-ups he liked to have at the café over the road from the tip.

You may as well tell me to cut out my heart, Dad replied theatrically. *What's the point of living if you can't enjoy a burger or a fry up with your mates now and then?*

He'd winked at me, and I'd grinned back. Mum didn't give up though. She said she was worried about him.

One evening, about six months before, when I couldn't sleep, I'd heard them talking downstairs. I crept over to the staircase to listen.

You really ought to see the doctor, Bob, Mum was saying. *You know you should.*

It's nothing, Dad replied. *Just a touch of indigestion.*

But it's hours since you've eaten anything.

I've swallowed a lot of air. Dad burped loudly and I had to stop myself from laughing.

But Mum wasn't amused. *This isn't funny, Bob,* she said. *You always want to turn everything into a joke. But this is serious.*

Violet interrupted my thoughts. "Hey, droopy drawers, we've got work to do. We're going to save the aquarium, remember?" She wiped her mouth and screwed up the burger wrapping. "It's time to do some serious planning."

For the next half an hour or so we talked about the campaign. Well, Violet did the talking really: I just nodded.

We agreed that we'd start work properly in the

office the following day, writing a letter to tell people about the aquarium's problems and our campaign to save it, and asking for their support. We could hand it out to visitors and email it to people on Stephan's mailing list. We decided to start an online petition and to write to important people like MPs and ecologists to ask for their help. We'd contact the newspapers too, of course – and local radio and TV. Violet said that we should set up a Facebook page and tweet too. She didn't think Stephan would have a Twitter account ("he'll probably think it's something to do with birds"), but she'd ask him.

There was lots to do and it needed doing urgently – even more urgently than we realised. When we got back to the aquarium Stephan told us a local developer had offered to buy it for a lot of money.

"What did you say, Uncle Stephan?" Violet asked.

"I said I'd consider it."

We stared at him horrified.

"But you can't sell the aquarium!" I cried.

Stephan looked at us miserably. "I'm sorry, Dak. But I might not have any choice."

20

I was on edge all evening and couldn't settle. "Are you all right, love?" Mum asked more than once. I said "yes" – but of course I wasn't. I was worried sick about what was going to happen to the aquarium ... what was going to happen to Dad.

The next morning I was through the aquarium doors as soon as they opened. Violet was already in the office, waiting for the computer to load. She'd Skyped her parents again the evening before, she told me, and tried to explain about the situation with the aquarium; but they hadn't really listened. Her mum had moaned about the state of Violet's nails ("She never lets me paint them when I'm at home"); her dad, as before, "only wanted to talk about his beetles".

"You'd think that as a conservationist he'd be interested in what we're trying to do, wouldn't you? But no, if it's not beetles, then he doesn't want to know." She glowered. "I hope they eat him alive, I really do."

I was used to the way Violet spoke about her dad by now, but I didn't believe she could really hate him the way she made out. (How *could* you hate your dad?) OK, he'd gone away for a while and left Violet and her mum, but now he wanted to come back. How could you hate someone for trying to do the right thing?

Our first job was to write the letter we'd planned.

"What exactly do we want people to do?" I asked.

"Well, we want them to … to … support us."

"Yes, but how?"

"They could sign our petition."

"What petition?"

"The one we're starting."

"Oh, right."

"They could get in touch with the council too. We could find out the contact-details of the Health and Safety men from Uncle Stephan. And they could write to their MP. That's what people do when they're unhappy about something. My mum's always writing to her MP."

"What does she write about?"

"Oh, you know: rubbish collection, recycling, street lights, badgers…"

"Badgers?!"

"Yeah, our MP said he wanted to kill badgers because they spread TB to cattle. Mum said he was an arsehole and she wrote to tell him."

I smiled. Now I knew where Violet got her straight-talking from. "Did he write back?"

Violet tossed her head. "Mum just got some standard reply from his office saying her opinions had been noted. Politicians never say what they really think and they never do what they say they're going to do. That's why you can never trust them."

I thought about this for a moment. "What's the point of asking people to write to their MP then?"

"It's just what you do," Violet said simply.

It took us most of the morning to complete the letter and then we showed it to Stephan. He put on his reading glasses and read it aloud back to us:

SAVE OUR AQUARIUM!

Dear Visitor

We hope you enjoy your trip to the aquarium and agree with us what a special place it is.

There are over 300 species of amazing fish and sea creatures here from all round the world. You can learn about their habitats and feeding habits, watch them swim and eat and listen to fascinating talks about them.

The aquarium is also vital for conservation. There are endangered creatures here and we have special breeding tanks that allow their babies to survive and grow. But now this is all at risk. The council has ordered expensive repairs – and the aquarium may have to close. We can't let this happen!

Help us save the aquarium and the lives of all of the creatures who live here. Please support our campaign by signing our petition. You can also write to the council at ▮▮▮ or call on ▮▮▮. You could even contact your MP!
Save Our Aquarium!

Yours truly,

Violet McGee and Dak Marsden,
SOAC (Save Our Aquarium Campaign)

Stephan took off his glasses and nodded at us. "'SOAC'…" He pronounced it like "soak". "That's clever, I like that." (SOAC had been Violet's idea – "It's an acronym," she told me.) "It's a good letter, very well written. Your teachers would be very proud of you." He sighed. "The problem is, though, it's cash I need right now, not people's sympathy. Sympathy doesn't repair walls."

Two rosy spots appeared on Violet's cheeks. "It's not sympathy, it's support, Uncle Stephan. And with support you can do anything. You'll see."

By the end of that morning there was a neat pile of letters on the reception desk. Next to it was a sheet of paper that read, *Petition: please support our campaign to save the aquarium* – and a pen.

Our next job was to send the letter out to people on the aquarium's mailing list. I wasn't sure it had one (Stephan wasn't the most organized person), but Violet assured me it did.

"It was one of the jobs he asked me to work on when I first arrived," she said. "Uncle Stephan doesn't know anything about computers. Old people don't. Can you believe the aquarium doesn't even have a Facebook page?"

As it turned out the list was a mixture of email and postal addresses. We decided that Violet would take care of the emails, while I sorted the letters to post. First of all, though, we had to persuade Stephan that this was a good idea and wouldn't upset his customers.

"They might think it's junk mail," he worried.

"They're interested in the aquarium, aren't they?" Violet asked.

"Well, yes."

Violet beamed. "Then they'll want to help us save it."

"It might even make some of them come and visit," I suggested.

"Exactamento!" Violet exclaimed – and so it was agreed.

Violet and I got busy. Working on the task lifted the gloom of the last few days. I felt useful and excited, like when I'd first got involved in feeding the fish with Johnny. Now and then we'd come across a name or address that made us laugh: Tanya Butt, Cat Pratt, Cherry Stone, Francis Large, misstwinkletoes@mail.com, abominablesnowoman@hotmail.com, biged@me.com.

There were about two hundred names on the list so it took us a while to get through them all – especially as Violet insisted on "personalizing" every email. "People are more likely to pay attention if the email is addressed to them personally," she said. "My mum always deletes emails that aren't."

So I set about replacing the "Dear Visitor" with their actual name in my best handwriting, before folding the letter carefully, stuffing it in an envelope, sealing it and sticking on a stamp for posting. It was slow-going, especially as I had to stop a couple of times to go and help Johnny with the feeding. When Violet finished her emails, she helped me with the letters, which speeded things up. It still took us the whole day to finish.

Johnny offered to post the letters on his way home. "Ya been working so hard, it's the least I can do," he said, giving us the warm smile he usually reserved for the fish.

Even Stephan seemed more cheerful when he came into the office at the end of the day. "You *have* done a lot," he said.

Violet frowned. "There's lots more to do yet, Uncle Stephan." But I could tell she was pleased – and so was I.

The most important thing, though, was that we were doing something.

21

The next day we wrote a letter to the council. Violet decided it should be a bit more hard-hitting than the letter to the public, so she ended it with: "Don't shut the aquarium. Don't sentence the fish to death."

"Are you sure we should put that?" The thought made me feel suddenly sick. "The fish won't die, will they?"

"Some of them might," Violet insisted. "If Stephan can't find them a new home."

Would Stephan find the clownfish a new home? I wondered. And if so, where? It could be anywhere, I thought again, panic rising as I pictured Dad swimming around a tank somewhere far away without me there to look after him.

"You have to say things like that to make people take

notice," Violet said. "It doesn't matter if it's true or not. It *could* be true, that's the point. And it sounds dramatic."

I nodded, feeling calmer. Violet was just being Violet. Nothing was actually going to happen to the fish.

Next we wrote a letter to our MP. We asked Stephan who it was, but he didn't know, so we researched it online.

"Maybe he'll belong to the Green Party," Violet said. "They like nature. They'll care about the aquarium."

But our MP didn't belong to the Green Party – and *he* was a *she*.

"Oh, well, at least it's a woman," Violet said.

"Why's that a good thing?" I asked.

"Because women care more about nature and stuff. Men MPs like killing fish, not saving them."

I looked at her doubtfully. "Really? How do you know?"

"My mum told me. She says men MPs are a waste of time. They're never at their desks. They're always out shooting or fishing or having a really long boozy lunch."

"Don't women do that too?" I said. "Have long lunches, I mean."

"No, they eat a salad or a sandwich at their desk like my mum does."

"And they don't kill fish?"

"No, of course not! Only stupid men do that."

I still wasn't convinced. "I don't know any men who do that: my dad, Stephan, Johnny, your dad…"

Violet's cheeks flushed. "You don't know my dad! Why are you talking about my dad! I'm talking about MPs!" She glowered at me. "Sometimes, Dak, you're really annoying, do you know that?!"

And with that, she stood up and fizzed out of the room.

I sat stunned for a moment. What had I said that upset Violet so much? I went out into the foyer after her, but she was already pushing open the glass doors to the street. I was going to follow her, but Stephan stopped me.

"Let her go. Give her some time to cool down. She'll be all right in a while. She's like her mum – hot-headed, quick to take offence. Not always easy to get on with." He sighed. "What did you say to offend her?"

"I don't know really," I said. "I just mentioned her dad."

Stephan nodded. "Ah, that does seem to hit a nerve, doesn't it?"

I shrugged. "She says she hates him."

Stephan stroked his moustache thoughtfully. "She doesn't of course. She just hasn't got over him leaving.

She's hurt. It's almost like she's, well, grieving." He winced. "I don't mean like you, Dak…"

"I'm not grieving," I said quickly. "And anyway, her dad wants to come back, so she's got nothing to grieve about. She should be happy."

Stephan raised his thick eyebrows. "If only it were that simple."

I took a break from letter writing and went down to see Dad. This was the first time Violet and I had fallen out since the day of her arrival – which, given how touchy she could be, was quite an achievement. I walked into the room where the clownfish tank was … and froze.

One of the teachers from my school was there!

She was with a small girl, staring into Dad's tank. "Look, Mummy – Nemo. Look!" the girl squealed.

Luckily the teacher was facing away from me, so I slipped back into the room I'd come from. Had she seen me? I didn't think so, but my heart was beating hard and fast as I hurried away. If I was found out now everything would be ruined. I'd have to be more careful.

When I was sure the teacher and her little girl had gone I went in to see Dad. He was all action today, his little flippers waggling and his head with its white Alice band bobbing up and down and from side to side. The way he was flipping around drew attention to the white triangle at his middle, which, I noticed for the first time, looked like a pair of pants. A fish in pants! For a moment it all seemed too weird.

"What are you doing, Dad?" I said.

"What does it look like? I'm dancing!" he replied breathily and wiggled his belly. "I reckon I could be on one of those TV dance shows. You know, like *Strictly Come Dancing*." He waggled and bobbed more crazily than ever.

I shook my head. "You hate those shows, Dad; it's Mum who loves them. 'Come Prancing', you call it."

"Nonsense! You've got it all wrong. I love dancing, me." The clownfish shimmied to the right and then to the left.

I felt suddenly dizzy. Everything was flickering like a faulty light bulb. I shut my eyes to steady myself and when I opened them again, Dad seemed to have calmed down.

"Do you remember, when I was small, you used to put your pants on your head and do a mad dance around the room to make me laugh?" I said. The clownfish stared out silently with its small black beady eyes. "You remember, Dad?" I felt a prickle of unease.

The clownfish continued its silent, empty stare.

Then all of a sudden it wagged its head furiously. "Course I do! How could I forget the famous pants-on-head dance?" Dad wobbled and wiggled in a vague impression of the crazy dance.

I laughed, feeling closer to him than ever. Nothing could come between us.

"Now, you don't see that on 'Come Prancing', do you?" he chuckled.

"No," I agreed, chuckling too.

"I thought I'd find you here."

My laughter died in my throat and I turned round stiffly to see Violet standing there.

"You made me jump," I said. *How long has she been there?* I wondered anxiously. Had she heard me talking – laughing?

"You really like that Nemo fish, don't you?" Her tone wasn't exactly friendly but she couldn't have discovered my secret. If she had, she'd have let me know. Violet always spoke her mind.

"It's called a clownfish," I reminded her. "And, yes, I do. It's my favourite fish."

We stood next to each other peering into the tank.

"No, I can't see the appeal," Violet said at last. "Give me the piranhas any day."

22

We didn't talk about what had happened earlier – we went back to the office and finished the letter to the MP, then we showed it to Stephan. We discussed whether he should sign it, but we decided in the end (well, Violet decided and Stephan and I agreed) that it would be better coming from us as the campaign organizers.

In the afternoon we turned our attention to the press. Stephan had a list of contacts at local radio stations, newspapers and magazines.

"You could make a few changes to your letter and send it out as a press release," he suggested. "I'm sure you'll get some interest."

"I could do that!" I said enthusiastically. "We had to write a press release in English as part of our persuasive writing."

But Violet was against it. "Press people must get loads of stuff every day," she argued. "They haven't got time to read it all. We need to talk to them directly. On the phone."

My heart sank at this. I really didn't fancy phoning up radio stations and newspapers. But I needn't have worried, because Violet *did*. Of course she did. I remembered how much she'd loved talking to Mr Hoskins, how convincing she could be... This was a task made for her. And she couldn't wait to get started.

I looked online for press contacts that weren't on Stephan's list and checked phone details for those that were. But it was Violet who did the real work. She was amazing. You'd never have known she was a twelve-year-old girl, I thought, as I listened to her on the phone. She made the closing of the aquarium seem like the most important story ever – and she wouldn't take no for an answer. If she couldn't get the person she wanted she'd ask to speak to someone else – and if that didn't work she'd leave her number and demand that they called her back.

It was tiring just watching and listening to her, but exciting too. I loved the way she'd talk really seriously with someone over the phone one instant and turn to me with a huge grin the next. By the end of the afternoon she'd made about thirty calls. She'd had some interest, but looked a little disappointed.

"You were awesome," I told her.

"I know," she agreed.

"Why are you looking like that, then?"

Violet wrinkled her nose. "I suppose I was hoping for something more … major. A story or a feature or something."

"Maybe they just need time to think about it," I suggested.

"Maybe." Violet nodded, but she didn't sound hopeful.

23

When I was almost home, I saw Mrs Baxter come out of the house and I ducked behind a car so that she wouldn't see me. She'd only want to question me about the other evening when I'd avoided her. I hoped she hadn't mentioned it to Mum, but I knew she would have done. She couldn't help interfering.

Before going into the house I stopped to straighten Becks's boater, which had slipped forward over his eyes. It gave me an idea. What if I got a pair of Dad's old glasses and put them on Becks? It was just the sort of thing that would make Dad laugh. I'd give it a try later.

Mum was waiting for me in the hallway. She was dressed in a pair of black jeans and a yellow flowery top. Her light brown hair was tied back in a ponytail the way it always used to be and she was wearing the silver heart earrings that Dad had given her last Christmas (*No,* he'd said when she'd unwrapped the present, *they didn't come from the tip.*). She looked more herself – less pale, though she still had dark semi-circles under her eyes.

"Where've you been, Dak?" She sounded worried.

"At the aquarium. I told you this morning before I left."

"What? You've been there all this time?"

I shrugged. "We had a lot of work to do. We're running a campaign to keep it open."

Mum smiled. "That sounds interesting. Come and tell me about it, while I make dinner."

In the past Mum had always known just what was going on in my life, but recently, since Dad had … changed, we'd hardly talked at all. I'd told her that I was helping out with looking after the fish, but I hadn't talked about Violet, for example, or even Johnny really. There were lots of gaps to fill in. I wasn't usually much of a talker but now the words spilled out of me.

"Violet sounds like a handful," Mum remarked, as she stirred a pan on the stove.

"She's got a temper," I said. "But you should hear her on the phone. She's incredible. We're trying to get the newspapers and radio to support us. We can't let the aquarium close – or be sold." I shuddered at the idea.

"No, that would be a shame," Mum agreed. She turned to face me and her eyes had their old spark. "Your dad loved that place."

"I know. That's why we've got to save it."

We sat at the kitchen table together and ate spaghetti with a creamy tomato sauce – my favourite meal. There was ice-cream too. It was great having Mum back like this, so normal.

"You must miss Dad terribly, Dak," she said suddenly. "I do."

"It's OK, Mum," I said, scared she might start crying. "I think about him a lot – things he said, things he did. It's like he's still here."

I looked up from my bowl to see Mum's eyes fixed on me with sad concern.

"It's all right to cry, you know, Dak. It's all right to mourn. You don't have to keep it all inside. You don't have to pretend everything's fine, because you're afraid you'll upset me."

I shook my head. "No, I know, Mum. But honestly I'm fine."

Mum didn't look convinced. "Mrs Baxter said she passed you in the street the other day and you looked terrible. She was really worried about you."

"I wasn't feeling well, that's all. It's nothing to worry about." I smiled. "Mrs Baxter exaggerates."

Was this the moment to tell her? I thought. Now that she seemed so much better? Now that she'd be able to take in the news? Was this the moment, at last, when I could share my secret? For an instant I was tempted and felt a rush of relief.

But it quickly disappeared as I realised I couldn't. Because now that she was herself again, so much stronger and more normal, I knew she wouldn't believe what I'd tell her. She'd think I was making it up. She'd feel sorry for me.

I should have told her about Dad before. Now, it was too late. It would have to go on being my secret.

After dinner Mum insisted that I had a bath. She frowned when I took off my T-shirt. "You're so thin, love," she said. "Are you sure you're all right?"

"I'm fine, Mum."

She sighed. "I've neglected you badly, haven't I?"

I shook my head emphatically. "No, Mum. You weren't well. You needed looking after."

She stared at me, up and down. "Well, now I'm look- ing after you. And you'd better give me those clothes for a start. They look grubby. How long have you been wearing them?"

I glanced down at my black t-shirt and blue jeans. How long *had* I been wearing them? I couldn't actually remember the last time I'd worn anything else.

"I'll get a wash on tomorrow." She put her hand softly against my cheek. Then she said something that made my stomach lurch, "I'd better put your uniform in too. I think it's time you went back to school."

I slept deeply that night, but woke up in a sweaty panic, my heart hammering in my chest, and reached for the sweatshirt under my pillow. I pulled it out and held it tight against my face. I kept thinking about Dad all alone in a strange tank. About him without me, me without *him*...

I breathed hard into the sweatshirt as if it were an oxygen bag. Gradually I started to calm down. "It's all right, Dad," I whispered. "It's all right. I won't let them take you."

Suddenly I had an idea. If the aquarium did have to close, well, Dad could come and live here with Mum and me, couldn't he? I could set up a tank in the living room and we could sit together and talk and watch TV as a family like we used to. Dad could make us laugh like he always did, like he still made me laugh in the aquarium. I knew how to look after him – what food he needed, how to keep the right temperature and oxygen levels. If the aquarium shut then Stephan wouldn't need the equipment any more, would he? Surely he'd let me have some of it. I wouldn't need much. Then I could look after dad at home.

Everything would be fine. There was no need to panic. Dad was safe, Mum was so much better at last and the campaign to save the aquarium was up and running. OK, it hadn't achieved much yet, but at least we were doing something and even if it didn't work I had a Plan B.

I got up and looked for my clothes on the chair by the door where I always left them. But then I remembered Mum had taken them to wash. *How dirty had I looked?* I wondered. *Had I smelt?* No, I was sure that Violet would have told me if I had. I put on a pair of grey tracksuit trousers and a blue t-shirt that Dad had bought me. It had a picture of Bruce, the crazy shark from *Finding Nemo*. He was grinning toothily and blowing out a speech bubble saying, *I am a nice shark, not a mindless eating machine*. The T-shirt was a bit small for me now, but I liked it and I thought it might make Dad smile.

* * *

I crept downstairs quickly and quietly, trying to avoid Mum. After what she'd said the night before, I was worried she'd insist on talking to me about school – and that was the last thing I wanted. There was a little pile of post by the front door and I picked it up and shuffled through it, just checking there was nothing from school. There wasn't. Mostly it was junk mail – takeaway menus, estate agent flyers, charity leaflets. The headline on one of these caught my eye: Sponsor a Donkey!

I wasn't especially interested in donkeys, but it got me thinking. The leaflet explained that by paying a certain amount of money a year you could sponsor a particular donkey in a sanctuary. *That* interested me. What if we did something like that at the aquarium? We could ask people to sponsor a fish. They could even give the fish a name if they wanted. There were hundreds of fish in the aquarium. Supposing people sponsored a fish for £5 or £10, we could raise lots of money!

I stuffed the leaflet in my pocket and raced out into the street.

24

Violet had a money-making idea of her own and was talking to Stephan about it when I arrived. She wanted the aquarium to have a shop. All tourist attractions had shops, she said – and she was right, I thought. Whenever we went on a school trip there was always a shop to spend your money in.

Violet couldn't understand why the aquarium didn't have one already. Stephan said the aquarium was small and he'd rather use all the space for the fish than have a shop full of gifts that no one really wanted to buy.

"But you don't need to have a large shop, Uncle Stephan, and you don't have to sell tacky stuff," Violet insisted. "You could sell nice things – educational things."

"But where would I put a shop?" Stephan said.

"Right out there in the foyer. There's plenty of space."
Violet was looking determined. "It's the perfect place.
Everyone would see it when they came in and out."

Stephan was still doubtful. "What do you think,
Dak?"

"I think Violet's right. You'd definitely make money."

"And you need to make money," Violet reminded
her uncle.

Stephan stroked the barbels of his droopy moustache. "You may have a point," he conceded. "We'd
have to sell the right products, though."

"Of course," Violet said. "I'll choose them for you if
you like." She sounded so grown-up and professional.

Stephan sighed. "Go ahead, Violet. But it's going to
take time, isn't it? And time is one thing we don't have."

A heavy gloom fell on the room. It was the moment
for me to reveal my idea...

This time Stephan was much more enthusiastic. He
loved the idea – it would be a great way of getting
people more involved with the aquarium, he said, and
teaching them about the fish ("And raising funds,"
Violet pointed out) – plus, we could start almost
straight away. Violet offered to put together a leaflet on
the computer, if I helped her with the wording. In just

a few minutes the mood in the office had lifted again.

"Well *done*, Dak," Stephan said.

Just then the phone rang. Violet answered it. She listened for a moment, then, "Yes, this is Violet McGee speaking."

The conversation that followed was brief and Violet hardly spoke. She said "goodbye" then pressed the button to end the call and almost threw the phone down on the desk. When she turned to face Stephan and me, she had a huge smile on her face.

"That was the local radio station. They want to do an interview this afternoon!"

"Wow! That's amazing!" I said.

"Wonderful news!" Stephan agreed. He smiled thoughtfully. "We'd better think about what you're going to say."

Violet shook her head and her blonde fringe flopped over her eyes. "I'm not going to say anything, Uncle Stephan." She pushed back her hair and stared at me. "Dak is."

25

I protested of course. Violet would be much better at doing an interview than I would. It was just her sort of thing. I'd panic and stutter and not know what to say. I'd be hopeless, I said.

She wasn't having any of it. Usually, she told me, she'd be the best person to speak. But when it came to fish, it had to be me. "When you talk about them you come alive. You've even managed to win me over. Before I met you my only interest in fish was whether the batter was crispy enough."

I was flustered. "But what shall I say?"

"Tell them about how amazing fish are and why you love them so much and what's so great about the aquarium and how the council are going to close it down unless we can raise enough money to pay for the repairs.

Tell them about our campaign and what people can do to help. And, most important of all, don't forget to tell them about your brilliant idea for sponsoring fish."

It sounded easy enough when Violet said it, I thought. But then nothing threw her. I was just an ordinary, shyish twelve-year-old boy; she was a phenomenon, who'd phoned my headteacher and pretended to be Mum. *My headteacher!* The realisation struck me like a boulder.

"I can't do it, Violet!" I said. "I can't do the interview!"

"Of course you can, Dak. You'll be fine," she tried to reassure me.

"No, I mean I really can't do it. I'm supposed to be in the country, remember. You told Mr Hoskins on the phone."

"Ah," Violet muttered. For once, it seemed, she was lost for words. But only briefly.

"I didn't say how long you were going to be away, did I?" she said triumphantly. "Anyway, your head'll be in school, won't he? So he won't hear it." She beamed at me as if what she'd said was impossible to contradict.

"I suppose so," I shrugged.

I worried about the interview all morning. I rehearsed it with Violet, like we had the conversation with Mr Hoskins, but this was totally different, a lot more challenging – for me anyway, as I was the one who had to come up with the answers.

I went down to see Dad to tell him about my radio interview (but not exactly what it was about – I didn't want to worry him). I said I was going to talk about the aquarium and asked if he had any tips he could give me, but he was too preoccupied with practising for his race with the damselfish to stop and talk. All I got was a quickly bubbled "Dignity. Don't forget your dignity." He didn't even stop to look at my T-shirt.

Johnny was more helpful. "Tell 'em about the seahorses – people love that sort of thing," he advised. He gave me a grin that I supposed was meant to be encouraging. "You'll be fine, mate," he assured me. "You been learned by an expert, ain't ya?"

The radio station sent a car to pick me and Violet up. I was glad she was coming with me. She'd painted her nails purple – her "lucky colour" – to celebrate my interview.

I wasn't celebrating. I had a last try at persuading her to take my place, but she wouldn't, of course. She wasn't one to change her mind once it was made up – and I knew it. I was just so nervous. It was like that awful stomach-flipping moment waiting for the whistle to blow for the start of the hundred metre sprint on sports day – only ten times worse. I felt really sick and my legs were so weak and wobbly I could barely walk when I got out of the car.

The driver led us into a reception area where we had to write our names in a book and were given visitor passes.

Violet was amused. "It's like being in school."

"Mmm," I agreed, but I was too tense to return her smile.

We sat on a sofa and waited to be collected. On the walls around the room were framed black and white photographs of famous people who, I guessed, had been interviewed at the radio station in the past.

"Next week they'll have a photo of you on the wall," Violet joked. When I didn't respond she rolled her eyes upwards, "Try to relax a bit, Dak. You're not at the dentist's."

I sighed heavily. "This is so much worse than the dentist's."

"*Nothing's* worse than the dentist's." Violet always had to have the last word.

A door opened behind the reception desk and a young woman appeared. She came over to us. "Hi, I'm

Theresa," she said with a friendly smile. "You must be Dak."

I nodded.

"And I'm Violet McGee," Violet announced confidently, holding out her hand for the woman to shake. "We talked on the phone."

The woman looked really surprised. "I didn't realise you were … so young. You sounded so grown-up on the phone. I thought you were an adult."

Violet beamed. "I know. Everyone says that."

But now there was a problem. Because we were both children, Theresa explained, we needed to be accompanied by an adult.

"Well, you're an adult," Violet said bluntly. But apparently there was more to it than that. We needed our parents' permission.

Violet frowned. "My parents are both in Africa and Dak's—"

"My Mum's ill," I interrupted. "You can't talk to her."

I didn't know why I said that exactly. She was a lot better now, but I didn't want her involved.

"And his dad's dead," Violet added.

"Oh, I'm sorry," Theresa said. She looked a bit embarrassed.

For a few minutes I thought I was off the hook and the interview would have to be cancelled. But Theresa spoke to Stephan and told us it was going to be OK. She was emailing over a document for him to sign and scan and send back.

"He'll never be able to do that without me helping him." Violet sighed as we sat and waited on the sofa. But she was wrong, because minutes later Theresa was back smiling.

"All sorted," she said. She led us to the doorway she'd just come through and along a corridor. She stopped at a door with a red light shining above it.

"That means we're on air," she explained. She looked at Violet. "You can sit in the control box with the producer while Dak's being interviewed." Then, as if she'd worked out what Violet was like, she said, "You'll need to be very quiet."

Theresa took Violet in then came back for me.

"Victoria's going to be interviewing you," she told me. "Hopefully there'll be lots of people listening." She must have seen the terrified look on my face, because she gave a half-laugh before continuing, "It's nothing to worry about, Dak. Victoria's very good at this. She'll help you if you get stuck at all, but I'm sure you're going to be fine. I'm certainly looking forward to hearing what you've got to say." Her smile was so warm and encouraging that I immediately felt a little better. "Cool T-shirt by the way. *Finding Nemo*, right?" I nodded. "I love that film," she said.

We went in when there was a music break. The song was an old one I vaguely recognized – something Dad had listened to perhaps? Victoria was sitting behind a round table and she got up and came over to greet me.

"Pleased to meet you, young man," she said, holding out her hand. I shook it weakly. Victoria was older than Theresa, about Mum's age, I thought. She had shoulder-length dark hair that was peppered with grey and her eyes were an amazing blue, almost violet. She led me over to the table and pointed to the chair I was to sit on. She handed me a set of headphones and helped me adjust them so that they fitted over my ears.

"How's that? Comfortable?' she asked. I nodded. (Actually they felt a little too big and heavy – more for a grown-up – but I didn't want to make a fuss.)

Theresa pointed to a microphone on the table in front of me. "Just speak in your normal voice," she told me. "The guys in the box'll make any adjustments necessary." She waved her hand towards the control box and, looking across, I saw Violet staring out at me through the glass. She raised a thumb and I smiled nervously.

"Good luck then," Theresa said – and she turned to go.

"Shouldn't you say, 'Break a leg'?" I asked.

"I hope it won't come to that." She laughed as she walked out of the room.

When the music came to an end, there was a traffic announcement. Then Victoria nodded at me.

It was time for the interview to begin.

26

"Now, it's my very great pleasure to introduce to you a young man who's passionate about fish," Victoria began, glancing at a screen in front of her. "His name is Dak Marsden and he's just twelve years old. He's also the coordinator of a campaign to save our local aquarium from closure – or joint coordinator, I should say, with his friend Violet McGee, who's also twelve." She looked up and across at me. "Welcome to the programme, Dak."

I nodded – then remembered this was radio!

"Hi," I said – my voice was strangely high and croaky in the headphones. Was that really how I sounded?

"Now, Dak," Victoria continued, "before we talk about the campaign, I'd be really interested to know – and I'm sure our listeners would too – how your passion for fish started and what it is that you find so fascinating about them."

It was the perfect first question. As Violet had said that morning, fish was the one thing I loved talking about. It all started three years ago, I said, when Dad took me to the aquarium. I explained that he loved fish too and we often went together. I told her about that first magical visit, how I'd been hooked from the moment I'd looked in a tank and seen the rays flapping. "They were amazing," I said. I told her how Dad called them "rays of sunshine" and I talked about some of my other favourite fish: the lionfish, the long-horn cowfish, the beautiful jellyfish and, of course, my absolute favourite, the fabulous clownfish.

"And do you still go with your dad?" Victoria asked.

The question totally threw me. I gawped at her, panic rising. My mind was suddenly a chest of empty drawers.

"N-no, he's…" I stuttered. I was going to say, "He's there," but I stopped myself just in time. "He's … not here anymore." I could feel my face burning and my heart was beating like crazy.

Victoria must have realized something was wrong because she quickly changed the subject and moved on to ask me about the campaign: How did it come about? What did I hope it would achieve? Was there anything that listeners could do to help? I managed to pull myself together and give the answers I'd practised with Violet earlier. I even mentioned the seahorses. Victoria really liked my sponsorship idea and said it should be a "priority cause" for her listeners. She urged them to get in touch right away.

By the end of the interview there had already been several calls, emails and texts promising support, Victoria told me. "It seems like there are a lot more people out there who care about fish than you might think," she said, before wishing me and my campaign all the best. Then it was time for more music and Theresa reappeared to take me back to reception, where Violet was waiting.

Her usually pale cheeks were flushed. "Good job!" she exclaimed. "We're going to raise lots of money from this." Her eyes sparked with excitement. "I told you you'd be fine, didn't I?" She grinned and shook her head. "Well, I was wrong. You were fabuloso!"

The ride back to the aquarium was a lot more fun than the ride there. I felt good, really good. I'd never have dreamed I'd be able to talk like that to a total stranger – and on a live radio show! I'd spoken clearly and with, well, dignity. Dad would have been really pleased, I thought. Dad *would* be really pleased when I told him about it later.

As it happened, Violet was thinking about Dad too. "Why didn't you just say he was dead?" she demanded. "I mean it's the truth, isn't it, and I think it would have got us even more support."

I frowned. "That's why I didn't say it. I don't want people's pity, Violet. I don't need it." *I don't need it because my dad's not dead*, I might have continued, but I didn't. That was my secret – and mine alone. No one else would understand. It was my duty to keep that secret – and Dad – safe.

Stephan was waiting for us in the foyer and gave us a round of applause. "Outstanding!" he congratulated us. He'd had the radio on in the office, he said, and when the interview had come on he'd played it over the public address system so that everyone in the aquarium could hear. "You went down a storm. Take a look at this." He held up the petition sheet which was full from top to bottom with names and signatures. "I've had to start a new sheet," he said happily. "And I've had two newspapers on the phone wanting to do interviews. One of them is going to turn it into a proper full-page feature."

"That's great, Uncle Stephan!" Violet yipped.

"And it's all down to you, Dak," Stephan said.

I shook my head. "No, it's down to *us*. None of this would have been possible without Violet." I grinned at her and she grinned back. We were eco-warriors, campaigners – and best friends.

"I'm glad someone appreciates that," she said.

27

Doctor Doyle was in the sitting room with Mum, drinking tea when I arrived home. I knew at once from the look on their faces that I was in trouble.

"Dak," Mum said. It wasn't a greeting and she didn't smile.

"You'd better sit down, young man," said Doctor Doyle. Her face was stony.

"I had a phone call a little while ago from your headteacher," Mum said coolly. "He'd been contacted by a reporter wanting to know more about you. It seems you were interviewed on the radio this afternoon. Mr Hoskins was a little bewildered because he understood that you and I had gone away to the country. That's what I told him apparently. He also said he'd had a letter from Doctor Doyle informing him that you weren't well enough to go back to school." I felt my face burn. I dropped my head but I could sense the doctor's glare as sure as a searchlight.

"I think you've got some explaining to do, young man," she said sharply.

"Did you write that note pretending to be Doctor Doyle?" Mum asked.

I nodded. I glanced up at Mum then at the doctor. "I took the headed paper from your briefcase last time you came."

"Why would you do that?" Doctor Doyle's voice was as hard as the look on her face.

"I thought they'd make me go back to school. And I didn't want to go. I couldn't go. I wanted to stay with Mum, and —" I took a deep breath— "I thought that if they had a doctor's note then they'd leave me alone." I looked at Mum pleadingly.

"Oh, Dak," Mum sighed and she came over and put her arms around me.

Doctor Doyle wasn't so easily won over. She gave me a stern lecture about how what I'd done was a serious criminal offence, and I could be in big, big trouble if she were to report it. Did I understand that? I nodded. Would I promise that I'd never do anything like that again? I nodded again.

This seemed to satisfy her because she said she wouldn't take the matter any further. She didn't look happy though. I said I was sorry, and in a way I was – I was sorry that Mum had got drawn in and been upset – but I just couldn't feel guilty. None of what had happened would have been possible if I hadn't written that letter and Violet hadn't made that phone call to Mr Hoskins and I'd had to go back to school. What was it Dad had said? "Life is about getting your priorities right". Well, it felt like I'd done just that.

When the doctor had gone Mum began her interrogation. She wanted to know where Mr Hoskins got the idea that we were going on a holiday to the country.

"A friend of yours pretended to be *me*?" she said incredulously, when I told her about the phone call.

I nodded.

"Who?"

I squirmed. I didn't want to betray Violet – but I'd had enough of telling lies.

"It was Violet," I confessed, telling myself that Mum would never meet Violet, so it didn't matter.

"That girl!" Mum exclaimed. "She sounds like quite a character."

"She is," I agreed and I couldn't help smiling.

"So, is there anything else I should know? Anything else that I'm supposed to have told people?"

I shook my head. "No, that's it. I'm really sorry, Mum. I didn't mean to cause trouble. I just didn't want to go back to school and I didn't think Mr Hoskins would understand. I wanted to talk to you about it but…"

Mum shut her eyes for a moment. When she opened them, again they were full of tears. "I know, love. I haven't been … on top of things. I can see what a strain you've been under. But things'll be better now, I promise." She put her arms around me and drew my head in against her chest.

I breathed in her familiar sweet vanilla scent and it was like oxygen to my heart. I'd happily have stayed that way all evening, but Mum wanted me to tell her about the radio interview. So, at first hesitantly, then more fluently, I told her the story of my day.

"I wish I'd heard it," Mum sighed when I'd finished. "My son's a media star and I didn't get to hear his moment of glory."

I shook my head. "It wasn't that great, Mum. I was talking about the aquarium mainly." I remembered what I'd said about Dad and I was glad that she hadn't heard it.

Mum took my head in her hands and kissed my

forehead. "I'm sure you were brilliant. You *are* brilliant and I'm very proud of you." She let go of my head and grasped my hands in hers, her dark eyes gazing into mine. "And you know, don't you, Dak, that Dad would be very proud of you too." And when she said that, my day – which had already been amazing – was perfect.

28

The next day things went crazy. The phone in the aquarium office barely stopped ringing with people asking about the campaign or offering to sponsor a fish or wanting to talk to me. Violet set up interviews with a local newspaper and a magazine, one at the aquarium and one at home. Another paper wanted to send a photographer. Theresa from the radio station phoned to say that the feedback from my interview with Victoria had been incredible – they'd never had anything like it. The station wanted me – and Violet – to return in a week or so to report on how the campaign was going.

Violet was loving it. She was at the heart of everything – organizing, directing, playing the role of the campaign leader. She was so confident, so totally in control.

"They ought to interview *you*," I said. "You're much better at all this than I am."

"No, it's you they want to talk to, Dak," she insisted. "You're the one with the story."

"You've got just as much story as I have. Your dad's a famous entomologist."

"He's not famous. Well known in his field perhaps."

"Well-known entomologist, then." I shrugged. "He's not a binman."

"No, I know. But he's not—" She stopped suddenly, grimacing.

"He's not dead," I finished. Then I frowned. "Is that why they all want to talk to me?"

"No, no. They're talking to you because you're passionate about fish and saving the aquarium, but, well, you know how journalists are…"

"No, I don't."

"People are interested in stuff like that."

"Like what?"

"Like how you and your dad used to go to the aquarium together and then he died. And now you want to save the aquarium. I suppose they think you're doing this for him, because you loved him…" Violet's bright eyes pleaded with me. "Well, aren't you, a bit?"

"I suppose so," I agreed.

You've no idea just how much this is for my dad, I thought. *My dad's a fish – that's the* real *story*. But I wasn't going to share it with any newspaper.

I helped Johnny feed the rays later. I'd got the hang of the pincers now and the feeding was perfectly timed to Johnny's slick chat.

"Ya did good yesterday on the radio," he said afterwards.

"Thanks." I smiled.

"And ya remembered the seahorses."

"I listened to the expert," I said and Johnny nodded, the crab tattoo on his neck pulsing as if it was alive.

I wanted to talk to Dad about the radio interview. I thought maybe it was time to tell him what had been happening with the aquarium. It felt like we hadn't talked properly for a while. I also wanted to tell him that Mum was so much better. She'd agreed with Mr Hoskins that I could stay off school as there were only a few days left until the end of term.

The head wasn't at all pleased when he'd heard what I'd done but Mum managed to win him round. Lucky for me he really liked the aquarium – the school regularly took groups there. One of the conditions of me being allowed off school was that I had to write up the campaign, like a project, and present it to him at the start of the next school year. Which was fine by me.

There was a new fish in Dad's tank and it was stunning: bluey purple. It reminded me of Victoria's eyes. I looked to see if Stephan had listed it yet. "*Pseudochromis fridani*, **orchid dottyback**," I read, as the fish flashed by in all its brilliant glory.

"I see you've got a new friend," I said when Dad appeared.

Dad's tiny mouth pouted. "Flash Gordon, you mean. He's no friend of mine. He's only been in here two minutes and thinks he's the star of the show."

"He is beautiful, Dad."

"Gaudy, that's what he is. Gaudy. No class. No dignity."

I laughed. "You sound like you're jealous."

"Me, jealous? Of *him*? He's only a pseudochromis, for goodness' sake. Not even a proper chromis – a *pseudo*-chromis!" He waggled his tiny fins, as if in mock applause.

I started to tell Dad about the problem with the aquarium and our campaign to save it, but he kept getting distracted by the new fish. I didn't even get as far as telling him about my radio interview. I tried to get his attention, I really wanted to talk to him, but it was no use. He wouldn't look at me and after a while, he turned and wiggled after the dottyback. It seemed like he just wasn't in the mood for listening, so, in the end, I gave up and went back upstairs to see how Violet was getting on.

"Dak, guess what!" she exclaimed when I walked into the office. Her eyes were wild with excitement.

"What?"

"They want us to go on TV!"

I was stunned. "TV?"

"Yes, TV! They're sending over a reporter and a cameraman. We're going to be on the news!" She started to dance about the room. I stood there grinning. Then I joined in dancing too.

The TV crew arrived in the middle of the afternoon. There was a camerawoman and a soundman and a0male reporter, about Theresa's age, who was going to ask the questions, and a man called Ricky, who seemed to be in charge. Stephan suggested that they could film in the reception area (pointing proudly to the quotes on the walls) or, if they needed somewhere quieter, they could use the office? But Ricky wanted to film in the heart of the aquarium itself, he said.

Stephan wasn't sure at first. "It'll be fine, Uncle Stephan," Violet assured him. "I'll sort it out. Leave it to me."And sort it out she did, moving people away from the places where Ricky wanted to film and stopping them from making too much noise.

The reporter began by interviewing Stephan next to the wall that was the cause of all the trouble. This took a few takes as the soundman had some problems with the echoes. Then Ricky wanted some footage of the fish in their tanks, which Violet organized. Finally he wanted to interview me and Violet about the campaign.

"We need an interesting backdrop," he said. "Something colourful preferably."

Violet said she knew just the spot. I thought she might choose the piranha tank (even though you could hardly call the piranhas colourful), but she didn't. She chose the tank that was my favourite.

"Hello, son. Back again?" Dad mouthed when he caught sight of me. Then he saw the TV crew with their equipment and his mouth gaped. "Is that a TV camera?" he murmured. I nodded. Dad waggled his tiny flippers and wiggled his body. I chuckled.

"Hello-oo, Da-ak," Violet called. "The camera's

this way." Reluctantly I turned away from Dad. Violet smiled at Ricky. "Dak's crazy about fish," she said. "He could watch them for hours. Couldn't you, Dak?"

"Yeah. They're amazing."

"That's a clownfish, isn't it?" said Ricky, nodding at the tank.

"Yeah. All fish are great, but clownfish are the best."

I couldn't see Dad's reaction, but I imagined him giving a little dignified bow.

29

The interview went fine. Violet did most of the talking about the campaign and I spoke about the fish. The TV people wanted to know about Dad too – just as Violet had said they would. I felt uncomfortable talking about that, especially with Dad there behind me, but I did my best. It was for the good of the aquarium, I kept reminding myself.

"You're a very brave boy, Dak," the reporter said.

I frowned. She was like those people at the funeral, calling me brave. I didn't understand how I was brave. Surely you had to do something heroic to be brave – like save someone's life.

"Why?" I asked.

"Taking on this campaign to save the aquarium so soon after your dad died," the reporter explained.

I shook my head. "That's not brave. I just love fish, that's all." *And anyway*, I thought, *my dad hasn't died. He's right here.*

When the TV crew had gone, I went back to Dad's tank to have a chat.

He was bubbling with excitement. "So I'm going to be on TV!"

"Yes, Dad," I said. "We both are."

Dad quivered then seemed to droop a little. "My first time on TV and I'm not going to be able to see it. Just my luck."

"I'm sure Stephan will record it. And the TV people told us they'd send us a DVD so we can use it for our campaign."

"That's not much use to me in here," Dad grumbled.

"I can borrow a DVD player and play the interview for you. We'll watch it together."

This seemed to cheer Dad up for a moment. But then his mouth drooped again. "No one'll know it's me, will they? All they'll see is a bloomin' fish."

"A magnificent fish, Dad. A magnificent, wonderful, fabulous fish." I paused for emphasis. "A fish with dignity!"

"Dak?" The voice took me by surprise and for an

instant I didn't recognize it as Violet's. Then I turned. She was standing behind me in the shadows, watching, like that first day I'd met her. "You're talking to that fish." Her tone was unusually hesitant.

I said nothing. What was there to say?

"You called him 'Dad'," she continued, frowning.

I opened my mouth to speak, but no words came. My mind was whirring, like in the recording studio when Victoria had asked if I still went to the aquarium with Dad.

"Well, Dak?"

I glanced back at the tank, saw Dad's raisin-black eyes staring out as if urging me to reveal the truth. I looked back at Violet, taking a deep breath to steady myself.

"He is," I muttered. I half-turned and nodded at the tank. "That clownfish there, he's my dad."

Violet laughed uncertainly. "You're joking, right?"

I shook my head. "No, I'm not. He's my dad."

"Your dad's dead," Violet said bluntly.

I shook my head again. "He's not. He's … changed. He's turned into a clownfish." Finally I'd said it, shared my secret. And it came out almost matter-of-factly, not in the dramatic manner I'd imagined: as if it were the most obvious thing in the world. Because now, well, for me, it was. I felt lighter, relieved, like my head was full of air.

Violet laughed again, louder and harsher this time. Her eyes narrowed. "Don't be stupid, Dak. People don't turn into fish."

"My dad has. He talks to me."

"He talks to you?"

I nodded decisively. Violet huffed. "Fish don't talk, Dak. Don't be an arsehole."

"I'm not. It's the truth." I spoke confidently, but a pip of anxiety formed in my stomach.

"OK then, prove it," she challenged me. "Talk to the fish. Let's hear him."

I glanced into the tank. Dad was swimming round the dottyback. "He's distracted," I said, the anxious feeling growing.

"He's a fish!" Violet snapped. "And like I said, fish don't talk."

"*He* does." My voice was shaky now. This wasn't how it was supposed to be.

Dad flimflammed to the front of the tank as if drawn by our voices. Violet strode forward and crouched down a little until she was eye to eye with him.

"OK, Nemo, what have you got to say for yourself? Tell me, what's it like being a fish?" She cocked her ear towards the tank. "What's that, Nemo? Nothing to say? Let's try another question. What's the capital of America? No? Let's try something simpler. What's two times five? I still can't hear you."

"Don't!" I pleaded. "Leave him alone." She was ruining everything. Dad's little black eyes looked hurt and confused, as if he couldn't understand what was going on.

But Violet was relentless. "How about this one: can you blow bubbles out of your arse?"

She'd gone too far. "Shut up! You're being stupid!" I yelled.

"You're the one that's stupid," Violet hissed.

"I thought you'd understand," I said, shaking. "I thought you were my friend." My voice was rising, out of control. "But you're just a stupid, bossy, bad-tempered, selfish, horrible girl!" I was shrieking now. "I'm not the arsehole – or your dad. You are!" I pushed past her.

Moments later I was through the foyer, shoving the glass doors open and hurrying out into the street. I stumble-ran, my breathing clumpy, my head thumping, and didn't pause until I reached home. I whacked the battered boater off Becks's head, then fell on the front step and sobbed.

30

Mum brought me in and hugged me. She made me some hot chocolate, then she sat down next to me on the living-room sofa and got me to tell her what the matter was. I was calmer now – less upset, more angry. I told Mum that I'd fallen out with Violet but I didn't tell her why. I wasn't going to risk revealing that again.

"She always has to be right," I said. "I'm sick of it."

"Well, I suppose she'll be going home soon," said Mum.

"And good riddance," I muttered.

We watched the news together. The item on the aquarium was right at the end, in the local section. It only lasted a couple of minutes. The reporter introduced the campaign, there were a few words from

Stephan next to the dodgy wall, then a tiny bit of the interview with Violet and me.

"That was great, wasn't it?" said Mum afterwards. "And I was right – you were brilliant." She leant across and gave me a kiss on the cheek. I hadn't really paid attention – I'd been gazing into the background at the tank where Dad was just visible, dancing and shimmying, desperate to be noticed.

"And they gave out a contact number too," Mum added. "So hopefully you'll have lots of people phoning up to offer money."

I frowned. "Violet and Stephan can deal with that. I'm not going back while she's there."

Mum gave me a concerned look. "Oh, Dak. It can't be that bad surely?"

"It's worse," I said. And I wouldn't talk about it any more.

We spent the evening watching TV and talking. I told Mum about the quotes on the foyer walls. One was by an art critic called John Ruskin and another by someone called Doris Lessing – I asked if she'd heard of them.

"I've heard the names, but I couldn't tell you anything about them."

"What about D. H. Lawrence?" I asked and I recited his quote.

Mum knew more about him. "He wrote novels – and poetry," she said. "I remember studying one about a snake when I did my GCSEs."

"And Robert Lowell – have you heard of him?"

Mum shook her head. "You'll have to Google him. But tomorrow – not tonight. You need an early night and a good long sleep. You look exhausted."

It was true. I *was* tired. The last couple of days had been so full of emotions. I felt like my heart had been ripped and shredded.

I woke up in a panic. In my dreams Violet was a piranha, but a huge one, more of a shark really, with enormous red eyes and massive teeth – and she spoke like the Finding Nemo shark Bruce. "I'm having fish tonight," she growled like in the film and chased me, jaws snapping. I was worried she'd attack Dad and I was trying desperately to find him before she did…

Once again I reached for Dad's grey sweatshirt. I hugged it to me, burying my face in its yellow smiley, hoping some of its happiness might rub off on me.

I went downstairs and poured myself a glass of milk. I put a slice of bread in the toaster… Then it came to me: of course Dad wouldn't talk to Violet, not when she was being so horrible and rude. As I sat at the kitchen table munching my toast, I remembered how upset he'd been about people who'd turned abusive down at the tip. He hated it. So, no way would he respond to Violet when she was being so nasty. She'd probably go and tell Stephan and maybe Johnny too that I was talking to the clownfish and calling it dad. I could hear the sneering laugh in her voice as she said it.

Well, let her sneer. I'd trusted her and she'd betrayed me. I should never have let out my secret – not to her, not to anyone. I thought for a moment about my old friends, from my old life – Ruby and Tom. Would they have treated me the way Violet had? No, I was sure they wouldn't. Some friend she was.

In the morning, the phone kept ringing. I would've let the calls go to answer phone but Mum took them. She hadn't answered the phone for ages. It was a sign that she was getting better, I supposed. The calls were from reporters wanting to arrange interviews, but I told Mum I didn't want to speak to anyone.

"Tell them to talk to Violet," I said. "It's her campaign. I'm not part of it any more."

I tried to distract myself by going on the computer to find out more about Robert Lowell, or Robert Traill Spence Lowell IV, which, according to Wikipedia, was his full name. He was an American poet, born on 1 March 1917, died on 12 September 1977. He'd won quite a few prizes and was obviously important. I put in the quote from the aquarium-foyer wall: *I often sigh still for the dark downward and vegetating kingdom of the fish.* It came from a poem called "For the Union Dead".

I Googled it. It wasn't like any poem I'd ever read before and I didn't really understand it. But I could tell it wasn't a happy poem. It seemed to be about an aquarium in a place called Boston in America that the poet used to visit as a child, but now it was abandoned, its windows broken and boarded up, and it was going to be pulled down to build a giant car park. He called the fish "cowed" and "compliant". I looked the words up. "Cowed" meant sort of scared and bullied, and "compliant" meant obeying rules and always agreeing with others.

Was that what fish were like? I asked myself. Well, there was no way Dad was like that. Dad. What was going to happen to him? The poem made me more worried than ever. I remembered how I'd shivered when Stephan had first read out the quote and I felt the same now, having read the poem. It was like there wasn't any hope. Things changed, but for the worse – and there was nothing that you could do to stop it. The aquarium, the fish, wishes and hopes … they were no more than bubbles, burst bubbles.

The phone rang again. I couldn't stay in the house. I had to get out. In seconds I was through the front door and on my way down to the sea.

31

The water winked and twinkled, blue near the shore changing to green further out. The sunlight gave it a sheen like it had been laminated. Some little kids in blue polo shirts and white sun hats were having a picnic on the beach, their voices squeaky with excitement. A couple of seagulls squawked and pecked at each other. A sudden strong breeze gusted in from the sea and took my breath away as I scrunched across the pebbly sand.

The tide was still out enough to see the strange bumpy landscape beneath the cliffs. The lumps of chalk had formed into shapes: a pillow, a flour sack, a giant egg, a gravestone... I quickly looked away out to sea, where a small boat with a single white sail skimmed across the water.

I was reminded suddenly of a poem Dad used to recite (a poem, he said, that *his* dad had recited to him) when we were at the seaside. I could feel his strong arm around me, hugging me close, and the unusual seriousness in his voice as he recited the lines:

> *I must go down to the seas again,*
> *To the lonely sea and the sky,*
> *And all I ask is a tall ship*
> *And a star to steer her by.*

Dad didn't know who'd written the poem or what it was called. It didn't matter, though. The words were beautiful: so simple, so atmospheric, magical ... dignified. It had hope ... very different from that poem by Robert Lowell.

I wished that Dad was here now, that his arm really was round me, hugging me to him. I tried to take a deep breath but it broke into a shudder. Everything had changed so much, I thought, in the few days since Violet and I had sat in the hole in the cliff and started to plan our campaign. We'd been full of hope then. We'd thought that we could change things, that we could save the aquarium. And we *had* achieved a lot. We'd got lots of attention and even raised some money – but not nearly enough. We were still far, far from the ten thousand pounds needed, which meant that Stephan would have to sell the aquarium. It would go the same way as the one in Robert Lowell's poem – bulldozed by developers to build offices or flats or a massive car park.

Mum had said that Dad would have been proud of me, but why? I'd failed; I'd tried but I hadn't managed to save the aquarium, to protect Dad's home – and worst of all I'd betrayed him by telling Violet his secret and letting her make fun of him and destroy his dignity. What sort of a son *was* I? I wished that the sea would wash over me, take away my misery and pain and anger, set me free – free like a fish…

I sat for a long time huddled on the shore, watching the incoming tide, until the sky clouded over. Without the sunshine, the wind was chilly and harsh and I started to shiver. I stayed a little longer even then, not wanting to move or go home…

In the end the cold was just too much – my whole body began to shake, and I had to get up and leave.

Bare-headed and one-eared, Becks peered at me wonkily through a pair of Dad's lensless turquoise-framed glasses. In another mood I might have found it funny but now it seemed sort of pathetic and sad.

I did my best to straighten the glasses, but it was difficult with Becks's missing ear. The straw boater was lying upside down on the grass where I'd knocked it the day before. I picked it up and dusted it off gently before putting it back on Becks's head. Then I went inside.

I heard Mrs Baxter the moment I stepped into the hallway and I stopped, stiffened. I really didn't want to have to face her. I headed swiftly for the stairs but I was too late. Mum must have heard the front door open and she called out to me.

"Dak?"

"Hi, Mum," I said, hoping I might still escape. I really didn't want to talk to anyone and especially not Mrs Baxter.

"Where have you been all afternoon?" It was obvious from Mum's tone that she wasn't going to be brushed off. Reluctantly I walked into the sitting room.

Mum and Mrs Baxter were drinking tea. "I've been worried about you," said Mum. "Where have you been?"

I shrugged. "I went down to the sea."

"You've been there all this time?"

"Yeah."

186

"It's nice this time of year, isn't it?" Mrs Baxter said, her friendly tone taking me by surprise. "Warm, but fresh."

I nodded. Mum offered me some cake but I shook my head. I liked cake all right, but I wanted to get out of the room and be on my own.

"We were just talking about your television appearance," Mum said. "Mrs Baxter saw you."

Mrs Baxter beamed. "You were quite a star. And your friend… What's her name?"

"Violet," Mum said.

"What an amazingly confident girl," Mrs Baxter said admiringly.

"She's not my friend," I corrected her.

Mrs Baxter looked confused. "They've fallen out," Mum explained.

"Oh dear, I'm sorry to hear that," Mrs Baxter said. "I'm sure you'll make up."

I shook my head. "No, we won't." All of my anger and resentment rushed back. "*Never*." And I slouched out of the room.

32

I didn't know what to do with myself. My thoughts came in wild waves and I couldn't control or make sense of them. I had to do something, so I started to tidy up my room. It was a bit of a mess because I hadn't tidied it for ages and Mum hadn't been in any state to nag me like she usually did. I was picking stuff wearily off the floor when, buried under a pile of clothes, I came across a screwed-up piece of paper.

It was the note Ruby had posted through our letter box the day after the funeral. *You can talk to me any time*, she'd written. *I'm always here for you*. I felt a pang of guilt because weeks had gone by and I hadn't spoken to her – or Tom, or any of my friends. I'd been so busy with the aquarium and Dad and Violet – rude, bossy, spiteful Violet. I wondered for a moment how they were, what they'd been doing, what they were doing now... But thinking about it just made me feel even more weary.

I was putting some books back on the shelf over my desk when I came across something else: a small pile of greetings cards. I took them down to have a look. They were from my last birthday. The one at the top was from Dad (Mum and Dad always gave me separate birthday cards). *Happy Birthday, Son!* was the message, but it was the picture I was gazing at. It was a clownfish swimming away from its anemone. I never really paid attention to cards – I was too eager to open the presents that went with them – and I'd totally forgotten that this one, my last birthday card from Dad, had a clownfish on it.

I opened it up. Inside it read, *Wishing you a Wonderful Day* (only Dad had crossed out the first "W" and replaced it with an "F"). Under this Dad had added in brackets *and many more of them.* Then he'd written – well, scrawled – *to my favourite son with love for ever Dad xx.* I swallowed hard, trying to take everything in - the picture, Dad's words... *With love for ever*, I read – and read again, a lump in my throat the size of a baseball.

When Dad had written those words he could never have dreamed – none of us could – that it would be the last birthday card he'd ever give me, that in just a few months he'd be gone, changed, a clownfish in Stephan's aquarium. I wanted him to be here. Now. I wanted it to be like that moment in *Finding Nemo* when Marlin and Nemo are finally reunited and Marlin gives Nemo a fish hug and says, "It's OK. Daddy's here. Daddy's got you."

But this wasn't a film; this was real life. I thought about my idea of bringing Dad home and looking after him in a tank and realized how stupid and child-ish it was. Even if Stephan did give me some of his equipment I wasn't expert enough to use it properly. Hadn't I seen when Johnny had taken Violet and me on his behind-the-scenes tour just how much knowl-edge and expertise you needed? All the technology and science that was required to keep a tropical fish healthy and alive? I put the birthday cards back up on the shelf and got ready for bed.

I lay for ages wishing sleep would come, but closing my eyes only made my brain whirl. *Failure, failure, failure,* echoed in my head over and over. After a while I heard Mrs Baxter leaving, the front door shut, then Mum's footsteps on the stairs. She came into my room and over to the bed.

"You look so tired," she said with a sympathetic smile.

"I'm all right," I replied.

"You don't look it, love." She knelt by the bed and stroked my forehead. "I really am proud of what you did," she said, adding hesitantly, "and Violet too."

I scowled. Just the mention of her name made me prickle. Mum sighed. "She really has upset you, hasn't she?"

I nodded.

"I think she wants to make up with you," Mum said.

"I don't want to make up with *her*."

"She seemed … well, sorry."

I gaped at Mum. "You've seen her?"

Mum nodded. "She came round, when you were out. She wanted to see you. She said she thought she'd upset you really badly and she wanted to apologize."

I snorted incredulously. "Violet apologize? I don't think so! She only cares about herself."

"Well, she seemed genuine." Mum held out a small white envelope. "She gave me this to give to you."

I turned my head away. But Mum was insistent. "We all make mistakes, Dak. They say the hardest thing's to say sorry. But actually the hardest thing's to accept an apology when someone's really hurt you." She held the note out again, but still I wouldn't take it. A sudden thought worried me. "Did Dad ever hurt *you*?"

"Yes, and I'm sure I hurt him – though he'd never have shown it." She smiled, but her smile seemed sad. "Everything was a joke to your dad." I could see tears glistening in her eyes. "I suppose… I suppose…" She took a deep, unsteady breath. "Well, I wish sometimes he'd taken things more seriously."

I thought about Dad and the sea poem and the message of love on the card. "He could be serious sometimes," I said.

Mum nodded. "Yes, I know, love. Just not always when it mattered."

I thought more about that when I was on my own again. I remembered that conversation I'd overheard between Mum and Dad. *You really ought to see the doctor*, Mum had said. Dad had just laughed it off, but had there been something wrong with him? Should he have gone to the doctor? What if…? My thoughts became confused, drowsy. I kept hearing Dad, standing in the kitchen grinning, telling "Doctor, doctor" jokes. He loved "Doctor, doctor" jokes:

"Doctor, Doctor, I feel like a pair of curtains."

"Pull yourself together."

"Doctor, Doctor, people keep ignoring me."

"Next, please."

"Doctor, Doctor, I feel like a pony."

"Don't worry you're just a little hoarse."

"Doctor, Doctor, I keep seeing Donald Duck, Mickey Mouse and Pluto."

"Sounds like you're suffering from Disney spells."

"Doctor, Doctor, I've got a bit of lettuce sticking out of my bottom."

"I'm afraid that's just the tip of the iceberg."

When I woke it was dark and the rain was clattering against the window. There was a whoosh in the air like the sound of the sea.

Someone was standing over me by my bedside but I wasn't scared. I made out a fluorescent-yellow high-visibility jacket with grey reflective bands, dark trousers with two white hoops around the calves, big black boots…

"Dad!" I sat up excitedly. "You came back. I knew you would. I knew you weren't dead. I knew you couldn't be dead."

Dad stood there in his work clothes, looking down at me through the clear lenses of his tortoiseshell glasses. He smiled, but faintly, and shook his head. "I came to tell you—"

"That you're alive!" I cried. I leapt out of bed and threw my arms around him. He smelled of sweat and soiled plastic and the vegetably odour of old rubbish and I sniffed it in eagerly as if it were a heavenly aroma. "You're alive!" I didn't want to let go. Ever. But I felt him shifting, sliding from my grasp. When I looked up, his brown eyes were deep and intense. "I love you, Dak," he said. "Don't ever forget that. I love you. For ever." His face smoothed into a smile. "Even if you did call my classic motor a wreck."

I could sense Dad fading and was desperate to stop him. There was so much I wanted to say, so much I needed to understand. "I did what you said, Dad, with that interview. I did it with dignity."

He nodded. "I'm sure you did, Dak. You're a good boy." He was so pale he was almost see-through now. "Thanks for looking after Mum. Tell her I love her. Take care of yourself."

I clung on to him. There were things I had to know. "Why didn't you go to the doctor, Dad – when Mum said you should?"

He shrugged. "What would I have said? 'Doctor, Doctor, I've got a twinge in my chest'?"

I grabbed his arms. "Yes, why not, if you had one? You'd have made me go to the doctor if there was anything wrong with me."

Dad nodded. "You're right." His features were blurring now.

"Then why didn't you go?"

"Because … because I was scared, I suppose. I didn't want to hear bad news." He shrugged again and sighed. His voice was barely a whisper now. "And anyway, I knew what he'd say."

"What?"

Dad's voice was barely more than a breath: "Well, that's nothing, sir, I've got a skeleton in my closet."

He was just a faint glow now. "Dad. I need you, Dad. Don't go. Please."

I tried to hold on to him but it was no use: my hands were just clawing air.

33

When I woke it was dark and the rain was clattering against the window. There was a whoosh in the air like the sound of the sea. I sat up and lifted the edge of the curtain. Daylight grey as a ghost glanced in. Through the rain I heard the bleating of a seagull chick.

I was alone.

Turning away from the window I could see my bedroom was just as it always was. I lay down again and pressed my face into the pillow, one hand sliding underneath for the sweatshirt. It was there, but there was something else. My fingers touched paper and I pulled out an envelope – Violet's note. Mum must have slipped it under my pillow when she kissed me goodnight. I stared at it, caught between my trembling fingers. It was like I was holding a booby-trap bomb.

I didn't want to open it. I didn't want to open it. I didn't want to open it... I had to open it. I slid one shaky finger under the flap and tore it open.

Dear Dak,

I'm so sorry I upset you. I shouldn't have said those things. It was stupid, like you said. I know you're angry and I don't blame you. You called me bossy and bad-tempered and selfish and I know I can be all of those things. I don't understand exactly what you meant about the clownfish being your dad but it was horrible and unkind of me to make fun of you — and him. I was angry with my dad and I took it out on you and that was wrong. I'm really sorry.

You're absolutely the best friend I've ever had. It's not the same here at the aquarium without you. Uncle Stephan's miserable and so is Johnny. He keeps asking me about you and when you're going to come back. We've had lots more calls about the campaign, but no one's got the heart to carry on with it. It's all really sad.

My dad Skyped me last night. Stephan sent him a link to our interview on TV and he'd watched it out there in Africa! He said he was really proud of me and he asked me lots of questions about the aquarium and what we'd been doing — and about you. He thought you were amazing. He and mum are flying back in a few days, so I'll be going home. I hope we can see each other and make up before I go. I don't want us to leave things like this after all we've been through together.

I hope you're OK.

Lots of love (and apologies),

Violet xxxx

P.S. I've been talking to the clownfish — your dad — but he won't talk to me. I think he's missing you. You have to come back soon!

P.P.S. I miss you.

P.P.P.S. Forgive me PLEASE!

I read the letter several times, skimming backwards and forwards, my attention snagging on the same line: *I know you're angry and I don't blame you*. Was I angry? I had been. Just last night I'd said I'd never make up with Violet, hadn't I? But right now, I wasn't angry. I was tired, I was worried, I was sad...

You're absolutely the best friend I've ever had. Wasn't that the same for me? Ruby and Tom had been my best friends since I started secondary school and I really liked them, but it was different with Violet. No one else could make me laugh or upset me the way she did.

I'll be going home. I'd known she wouldn't be there for ever but I hadn't thought about her leaving, about my life without her, about the great hole she'd leave behind. But it was the P.S. that kept drawing me back, making my heart race: *I've been talking to the clownfish – your dad – but he won't talk to me. I think he's missing you...*

Of course he wouldn't talk to her; he would only talk to me. And now he was all on his own. I hadn't seen him for nearly two days. He wouldn't know what was going on. He'd think I'd abandoned him... I had to go to the aquarium right away.

I got out of bed and threw on my clothes. I almost

fell down the stairs in my haste. Then I was opening the front door and hurrying out into the damp street.

I ran and ran, the wind roaring in my ears.

The aquarium doors were still locked and I beat them with my fists. "Open up!" I shouted. "Open up!" I had to get to Dad. I had to get to him. What if he was sick? Or had something important to tell me? What if he'd been waiting all these hours, wondering where on earth I was – if I'd ever come back?

Stephan appeared from the office, looking confused. I watched impatiently as he walked across the foyer then fiddled with his keys, finally unlocking the doors.

"Dak, what is it? Are you all right?"

But I was already racing past him into the tunnel to the main hall.

On I ran, past the pike, grayling, barbel… Past the bream and the pollack and the mackerel, the skinny-tailed sturgeon and the sly conger eel… Past the ugly perch and the rays in their open-topped pool. Past the exotic fish with their strange names: the long-spined porcupinefish, the reef stonefish, the foxface rabbit-fish, the crown squirrelfish, the flashlight fish… Past the grim piranhas. Past the jellyfish floating like cello-phane parachutes. Past the tanks of brightly coloured tropical fish: the vagabond butterflyfish, the bug-eyed Picasso triggerfish, the stripey lionfish with its skirts and deadly spines, Peter's elephant-nose and the tiny cardinal tetra. Past the delicate, bobbing seahorses. On and on…

At last, breathless, I arrived at the large tank, where blue damsel-fish, green chromis and now the purple orchid dottyback flickered among reefs of rusty-brown coral. My eyes passed over them … and, there he was, my dad, the clownfish, rising from his fluffy white sea-urchin bed and waddling through the water: black beady eyes, pink nose, thick Alice-band ring of white, bubbles rising from his tiny pouting mouth. With relief I watched him swim to the front of the tank. It was fine. Dad was fine. He was alive and well.

"Dad!" I said. "Dad, I'm back."

He turned and flickered away, his fins fluttering like butterfly wings. I watched him circle the tank until he was back in front of me again.

"Dad. It's me, Dak. I've come back. Sorry I left you on your own for so long."

The clownfish blew out silent bubbles.

I nodded at the dottyback. "How are you getting on with Flash Gordon?" He wiggled but said nothing. "Have you had that race with the damselfish yet?

Did you win? Dad?" I leant forward and put my hands on the glass. "Tell me a fish joke. You know, like that one about the ray?" He turned and flickered away. My heart sank then rose again as he did a quick about-turn and swam back. "Wild thing! You make my heart sing," I sang, wiggling my own body in a kind of dance. The fish opened its mouth as if it were about to join in, but just blew out more bubbles. "Talk to me, Dad," I pleaded. "Please. Talk to me." The clownfish stared out, its eyes black and expressionless. Its tiny bottom fins rippled as if waving, but it said nothing. "Dad… Dad… Please." My sight blurred as I stared at Dad and saw … just a fish. A cowed, compliant fish.

I pressed my forehead against the glass, my eyes wet and blind, barely aware of the quick footsteps on the floor behind me. In an instant, arms wrapped themselves around me and a head pressed down on mine. I smelt vanilla. "He's gone, love," Mum breathed into my hair. I swallowed deeply, my tears moistening the glass. Then I beat my head against it, sobbing. The tank was coffin-hard, unyielding. I slumped and let myself be turned and taken into Mum's arms.

"I don't want him to be dead," I wailed. "I don't want him to be dead."

Mum's hug tightened. "I know, love. I know." Her

voice was shaky too. "But you have to let him go."

I glanced over her shoulder and saw Violet standing in the archway, her green eyes tearful too. I reached out a hand and she stepped forward and clutched it in her own fingers. Then my eyes squeezed shut once more and I howled and howled until it felt as if a whole sea was flooding out of me.

34

I cried for two days.

Mum sat with me for hour after hour, hugging me, offering comforting sounds and words. I slept cradled in her arms. We barely spoke – what was there to say? I knew she understood everything. We cried and cried together. I couldn't bear to be parted from her. I couldn't bear to be alive.

By the third day I felt totally drained, exhausted. The pain was still there, but no longer like an open wound, more like a scar that wouldn't heal. Violet called and I agreed to see her. She only stayed for a short while but it helped a little. The next day she came again. The day after that Johnny stopped by with a card (with a picture of fish of course). He hovered uncomfortably in the hallway and told me the fish were missing me. They weren't feeding as well as usual. I was sure it wasn't true, but I smiled because I knew he was only trying to make me feel better.

There was more talk about the aquarium the following day when Stephan showed up with Violet and a big bunch of red roses for Mum. She made tea and we all sat together in the living room. He had good news about the campaign, which he said was going well.

"We might save it yet," he said with unusual lightness. I guessed *he* was trying to make me feel better too.

"You've got something to ask Dak, haven't you, Uncle Stephan?" Violet prompted.

"Ah yes, I have," Stephan said. "Indeed I have."

I was worried for a moment that he might ask me to do another interview or something, but it was nothing like that.

"I'd like you to write something. Just a couple of lines—"

Violet jumped in, unable to contain herself. "About fish."

"About fish?" I repeated.

"Yes," said Stephan. "A quote – that we can put up on the wall alongside the others."

"That's such a lovely idea," said Mum. I couldn't think what to say. I just gawped at Stephan. *What on earth would I write?* I thought.

"Maybe you could write about the clownfish," Violet suggested hesitantly, as if she'd read my mind.

I shrugged. "I don't know. Maybe."

I thought about it for the rest of the day. It didn't exactly take my mind off things but it was good to be thinking about something fun, something creative – like when we'd been coming up with ideas for the campaign. I scribbled lots of things down then crossed them all out. Nothing was good enough. Nothing was quite right. I knew I didn't want it to be gloomy like that Robert Lowell quote. I wanted it to be happy. I wanted it to be something that would have made Dad smile.

Late that night, long after I should have been in bed asleep, the words suddenly came to me. I wrote them down excitedly and emailed them to Stephan.

The next afternoon Violet suggested we go for a walk down to the beach. I said "no" at first – I didn't think I was ready, but somehow she managed to persuade me. Well, that was Violet for you. On the way out we changed Becks's headgear, swapping the straw boater for Dad's favourite baseball cap. It was bright red with a white crown at the front. Mum called it his "King of Jokers" hat.

We went to a quiet part of the beach, near the hole in the cliff where we'd perched the last time, and found a large rock with a flattened head that we could sit on together. We were silent for a while, enjoying the breezy sunshine and the glittering sea. Then Violet said, "I didn't think you'd ever forgive me for what I did." She flicked aside strands of hair that the breeze had blown in her eyes.

I shifted slightly on the rock and glanced across at her with one eyebrow raised. "Who says I have?"

Violet's fierce eyes narrowed. "You'd better have." Then she grinned. "It's good about the aquarium, isn't it?"

"Mmm," I agreed.

"Thousands of people signed our petition and lots want to sponsor fish. They really care."

"You made them care," I said.

"*We* made them care," Violet insisted. "And you'll be pleased to know, Uncle Stephan's going ahead with my shop idea."

"Did he have any choice?"

Violet laughed. "No, not really."

I watched her, smiling. "It's good to hear you laughing," I said. I pictured her that first day I'd met her in Stephan's office. "You were so grumpy when you first came."

"Me?!" she cried with mock astonishment.

"Yes, you." And I laughed, really laughed, like I hadn't for days and days. "I'm glad you've made it up with your dad."

Violet nodded. "Me too."

Violet's dad had Skyped her a few times since he'd seen the TV interview and it seemed to have made a big difference. She talked about him now with real affection. It was a long way from when he'd been the "arsehole". She actually confessed that she was looking forward to seeing him again when she went home tomorrow. She hadn't totally forgiven him, she said, but she was willing to give him another chance.

"You'll be able to impress him with all you've learnt about fish," I suggested.

"Well, it'll make a change from beetles," Violet said.

The summer sunshine splashed over the rock and made the tiny silver specks in its surface twinkle. Violet looked across at me almost shyly. "I *will* miss you, Dak, you know."

"I'll miss you too."

"And I'll miss Uncle Stephan and the aquarium and the fish."

I smiled. "Especially the piranhas."

"Yes, the piranhas." Violet paused thoughtfully. "And the clownfish."

I nodded but I didn't speak.

"I wish I'd met your dad," Violet said. "He sounds amazing."

"He was. He was the best dad ever." I looked away out to sea, feeling suddenly tearful. Seeing a boat there, I felt Dad's arm around me, heard him reciting the sea poem we both loved. I started to recite it myself quietly, my voice trembling a little:

> *"I must go down to the seas again,*
> *to the lonely sea and sky.*
> *And all I ask is a tall ship*
> *and a star to steer her by."*

I explained to Violet about Dad and the poem.

"I know that poem," Violet said. "But a different version."

"A different version?"

Violet nodded. "My dad made it up. Do you want to hear it?"

"Yeah, sure."

Violet coughed and composed herself.

> *"I must go down to the seas again,*
> *To the lonely sea and sky.*
> *And all I ask is a bag of chips*
> *And a steak and kidney pie."*

She'd recited the poem with complete seriousness, but now she beamed, her bright green eyes sparkling with amusement and I couldn't help laughing again.

"Dad would've loved that," I said with a sudden rush of happiness. I could see the delight in his face, as if he were right there with us...

I put my hand in my pocket, remembering something. "*I* wrote a poem last night … for my dad. I pulled out a folded piece of paper. "It's only short."

"Let's hear it," Violet urged, squirming to get herself comfortable on the rock.

I smoothed out the paper and, after taking a breath to steady myself, read:

> *"Watch him waddle, flipper fins flapping,*
> *Bubbles of laughter rising wherever he goes:*
> *The clown prince of fish, my hero."*

Violet sighed. "It's lovely, Dak. Really lovely. It

makes you smile but it's also sort of…" She searched for the right word.

"Dignified?" I suggested.

Violet nodded. "Yes, I suppose. It's perfect."

"Stephan says he's going to get Toby to write it up on the wall in reception, in memory of Dad." I smiled. "So my name will be up there along with D.H. Lawrence and Robert Lowell…"

"Plus it'll actually make sense – unlike those other ones." Violet grinned revealing her two vampire-like fangs.

I shook my head. That was Violet for you, she always had to have the last word. But, this time, there was more.

"You know I'm going tomorrow," she said.

I nodded. It wasn't something I wanted to be reminded about.

"Well, I wanted to ask you a favour, Dak."

"A favour?"

"Yes."

"What?"

She pursed her lips, frowned. "I want you to come with me now to the aquarium."

I gasped. It was the last thing I'd expected. I felt a surge of panic. "I – I can't."

"Please, Dak. It would mean a lot to me. To go there together, one last time, before I leave."

I took a deep breath and shook my head.

"You wouldn't have to stay long. I'd just like to get a picture of us together – in the office. You don't have to go down into the aquarium."

That made me feel a little calmer. The office would be all right, wouldn't it? I could just go in, take a picture and leave. There was no need to panic.

"OK then," I agreed. "But only for a minute." She smiled. "Well, maybe two minutes."

35

I'd walked from the beach to the aquarium lots of times over the past weeks. But I'd never felt as shaky as I did now. As we went down the steps to the front doors, my pulse was going crazy. I had to stop for a moment.

"It's OK, Dak. Really," Violet said. She put her hand on my arm. "The aquarium's shut. We'll just go to the office, that's all."

She tapped on the glass but there was no one in the foyer. She reached up and pushed a button.

"What's that?" I said.

"A bell that rings in the office. Hopefully Stephan'll be there."

I hadn't even known there was a bell. But it must have rung all right because a moment or two later, the office door opened and a smiling Stephan appeared. He walked quickly across to let us in.

"Dak, how wonderful to see you!" he said warmly. "I wasn't sure Violet would manage to persuade you."

I glanced at Violet questioningly.

She looked a little guilty. "It wasn't just for me that I wanted you to come, Dak. Stephan's got something to show you."

I frowned. "Really?"

"Yes, Dak," Stephan said. "I want you to look up there." He pointed halfway up one of the walls. I looked and my heart leapt. Written in Toby's neat black script, the paint still wet, was my poem about the clownfish. And underneath it was my name: Dak Marsden. I stared, speechless.

"Well, what do you think?" Stephan asked.

"It's cool, isn't it?" said Violet. "No, it's more than cool. It's fabuloso!"

I nodded, smiled. "It is. It really is. Thank you, Stephan."

"It's a pleasure," he replied. "I think it's my new favourite."

I smiled even more at that. Maybe all those times that Dad had urged him to "cheer up" had finally had an effect.

"Now we can go into the office and take that picture," Violet said cheerily.

I followed her through reception to the office door. But she didn't open it. She stood aside and waved her hand at me.

"You first," she said.

I shrugged. "OK."

I opened the door and barely had time to take in the office's new arrangement with the furniture pushed back against the walls, when a shout of "Surprise!" filled the room and suddenly I was surrounded by people. The first person I saw was Mum. She came over and hugged me. "I'm so proud of you, love."

Johnny came over too and shook my hand. "You done really good, mate," he said.

I just gaped, bewildered. I had no idea what was going on. I looked around at Stephan and Violet. She was grinning.

"The aquarium's saved!" she whooped.

"And it's all down to you, Dak," Stephan added.

Between them Stephan and Violet explained that after our TV appearance, a man had offered to donate the money needed for the repairs. Apparently he had been hugely impressed by our "dedication", but it was my mention of Dad that had been the crucial factor.

He'd been moved to tears, the man said, and had decided he had to do something to help.

"The repairs are already under way," Stephan said. He stroked his moustache thoughtfully. "So your campaign was successful. Thanks to you and Violet, Dak, the aquarium is staying open."

"Thanks to Dak's dad too," Violet added. She glanced at me a little uncertainly, as if anxious that she'd said the wrong thing, but I gave her a reassuring smile. She was right. It *was* Dad who'd inspired me to fight for the aquarium.

The room was busy now with people getting bottles out of boxes and filling bowls with crisps. It looked like we were going to have a party.

"Who are all these people?" I asked.

"They're our campaign supporters," Violet replied. "Lots of them have offered to sponsor a fish."

"That was a great idea of yours," said Stephan.

I didn't respond because I suddenly caught sight of two people I knew. I almost didn't recognise them because I never would have expected them to be here. When they saw me looking at them they walked quickly over.

"Hi, Dak!" Ruby said. She giggled and threw her arms around me. "It's so good to see you."

"And you." I held her close and hung on to her with my eyes shut because I didn't want anyone to see my tears. When I opened them again, Violet was there. I wiped my eyes.

"This is my school friend Ruby," I said. "And this is Tom. He's my friend too … mostly."

Tom grinned. "Hi, Dak. We've missed you … a bit."

"And this is Violet," I said. "She's…" Violet's tree-frog eyes were wary, as if she was wondering what I was going to say. "She's—" I smiled— "Violet." Then she smiled too – not a big smile, but enough that I knew she was OK. She wasn't going to be unfriendly, like when she'd met me.

It was a special party, having all my favourite people there – well, all except Dad of course. At one point Stephan raised his glass and toasted him. Mum smiled at that. It was great seeing her back to her old self again, chatting and laughing. She was the one who'd invited Tom and Ruby and I was so pleased she had. It was like the glass barrier that had been there since Dad died had finally come down and my old life could join up with my new one – the world of the aquarium, of Violet and Stephan and Johnny. Of course I still missed Dad – I really missed him – but my life had somehow become whole again.

There was something I needed to do, though.

"I'm going into the aquarium," I said to Violet.

She frowned. "You don't have to, Dak."

"I do."

"Then I'll come with you," she said.

We slipped away quietly, leaving the party, and went through the tunnel into the aquarium. It was gloomy, because the lights were off, but just bright enough for us to see. I hadn't told Violet where exactly I was headed, but she seemed to know. It was obvious, I suppose.

The tank was very still when we arrived. There was no sign of the chromis or the damselfish, but we weren't here for them. The purple dottyback made a brief appearance before swishing behind some coral, but, of course, we hadn't come to see him either. We peered into the murky tank, waiting…

And, finally, the clownfish emerged, its white Alice band fluorescent in the gloom. It wiggled its way forward to the front of the tank, its little mouth blowing bubbles, until it was facing us – and we could stare into its black, fish eyes. But it didn't stop. It carried on swimming around the tank.

"Watch him waddle, flipper fins flapping," Violet

said quietly. "The clown prince of fish, my hero." I turned and she gave me a quick smile. "It's definitely my favourite fish now."

"You like it more than the piranhas?"

She nodded. "I still like the piranhas, though."

I smiled. Then I thought of something. "There's this bit at the end of *Finding Nemo* when Marlin's watching Nemo swim off with his friends on an adventure. Do you remember?"

Violet pursed her lips thoughtfully. "Sort of."

"He's scared of losing Nemo, of what might happen to him. But he knows he has to let him go. It's hard, really hard, but he has to let him go. 'Bye, son,' he says. But it's a happy moment. It's the end of the film. Nemo's going to come back." I paused, took a deep breath. "Dad's not coming back. I've got to let him go."

Violet put her hand on my arm like she had earlier outside the aquarium. Her bright eyes stared into mine as if encouraging me.

I looked up from the tank towards the ceiling and shut my eyes. "Bye, Dad," I whispered.

We stood quietly for a moment or two, then we went back upstairs together to join the party.

Author's Note

This book has truly been a labour of love. I don't recall now where the idea for the story came from (though I've always loved tropical fish and am a frequent visitor to the London and Brighton Aquariums), but I do remember reading the first chapters to my oldest daughter when she was in her final year at primary school. In the eighteen years it has taken me to finally complete this book, she has finished primary school, gone through the whole of secondary school, a gap year and university, taken an MA, started as an intern at an e-book publisher, worked her way up to become Publisher, begun a PhD – and launched her own publishing company.

And I managed this book! (Well, I did write quite a few others in the meantime…) I always liked the story and intended to write it, but somehow it got sidelined as other stories successfully jostled for my attention. Every now and then I would think about it and have new ideas about the direction the plot should take. But it was years before I returned to writing it – and there was much work to be done.

I am hugely indebted to my editor Caroline Royds for taking this book on with all its flaws, and working with such skill and generosity to help me enhance and transform it – a big thank you also to Becky Watson. I'm delighted that its publisher is Walker Books, where I worked for many happy years and who have published me so well over two decades. I'm indebted too to the support of my family, Jinny, Amy, Kit and Josie, to my parents, to my friends (near and far), fellow authors and illustrators and to my patient agent, Hilary Delamere, who must have wondered if this book would ever be written, never mind published!

Clownfish is my 100th book – fortunately they haven't all taken so long to write! It's dedicated to my dad, Chris Durant, who died at the end of 2016; which seemed particularly poignant as I was, at that time, in the middle of a major redraft of this story about a son's grief for the loss of his father.

So, for a number of reasons, this is a very significant book for me. I hope you've enjoyed reading it.